CHASE

COMPLETE SERIES

CHASE

COMPLETE SERIES

by Cassia Leo

http://cassialeo.com

CONTENTS

1

Money will make a person do crazy things; like standing in front of a hotel waiting to be picked up for your first job as a professional escort.

As much as I wanted to, I couldn't blame my roommate for this new gig. Shane Meadows introduced me to *Black Tie Escorts* after I lost my part-time job as a children's party clown three weeks ago. Shane was one of the most handsome guys I'd ever laid eyes on. When I answered the roommate-wanted ad in the *L.A. Times* and showed up to find Shane standing in the center of a tiny but gorgeous artists' loft, I thought I'd finally hit the big time. Shane turned out to be gay, dashing any hope of fulfilling all the hot fantasies I'd been casting him in. And two years later, I still hadn't gotten my big break in Hollywood.

Midnight in August was the perfect time to stand outside a hotel on Wilshire Avenue. The breeze lifted the stray hairs near my temples, tickling my skin and sending shivers down my arms. The downtown lights sparkled and leaped off the brass trash bins, the gleaming taxi, the glass entrance doors behind me. The lights were dizzying and comforting at once. Even though the city could be harsh, it had become my home ever since my parents decided that chasing my foolish dreams was cause for disownment.

"Miss Jacobs?" an elderly voice called softly from behind me. Harry, the doorman, ambled toward me holding out a folded piece of paper in his wrinkled hand. "A gentleman called and had this message for you."

My first thought as I reached for the note was that whoever the service set me up with had probably driven by the hotel and changed his mind when he saw me. He definitely would have found me attractive. I'd never had a problem securing modeling gigs for print and online work. But I was not runway material. Maybe this guy, who would be paying $5,000 for one night with me, was looking to get a bit more for his money.

I unfolded the note and read two words: *NORTH ENTRANCE.*

When I looked up, Harry was almost back at his station near the front entrance. He turned to face me again and nodded to his right: north. I smiled my thanks and set off toward the hotel's side entrance. I had only known Harry for thirty minutes, but he had already shown me ten times more kindness than my new boss at *Black Tie Escorts*: Jessica Broom.

Jessica was twenty-seven, just three years older than I was, and she already owned her own escort service. How she managed this, I didn't know, and I was pretty sure I was not allowed to ask.

I rounded the corner of the hotel into a narrow roadway leading toward an underground parking structure. A black Lincoln Towncar sat parked in the center of the narrow road, lights on and engine idling. I suddenly became hyperaware of my surroundings: the moths flitting around the security lights, the smell of

Chinese food wafting over the fence from the restaurant next door, the fluttering nervousness in my belly, and the pulsating sensation in my crotch.

As nervous as I had been anticipating this moment all day long, a part of me was excited. Jessica claimed this client requested me specifically because it was my first time. She didn't say he picked me because of my ravishing beauty, which was a bit disappointing. The fact that he chose me at all was enough to pique my interest and had me fantasizing all day about possible candidates: a famous actor, a politician, or a film director who would insist on giving me my first big role.

Jessica only dealt with high-profile clients. She claimed this client was as high-profile as it got.

The driver stared straight ahead as if I didn't exist. As I approached, the back door swung open. I approached slowly until I could see into the cabin. All I could glimpse was a pair of gray slacks and black wingtips.

"Have you worked for any other escort services or is this your first time?" a smooth voice asked. I couldn't see him through the veiled darkness inside the car, but his voice sounded familiar, like I had just heard it today on the television.

I didn't know if answering with the truth would make him doubt me, but I figured if he wanted a pro he would have chosen one of the other girls. "This is my first time," I replied.

"Come inside."

I stepped into the backseat and my breath caught in my throat. My first client was Senator Chase Underwood.

Presidential candidate Chase Underwood. The gorgeous 39-year-old playboy who just settled down with his new wife last year.

His gaze glided over me, taking in every inch of my black dress and nude heels.

"Shut the door," he commanded, his voice gentle but confident.

I turned around to pull the door closed and when I turned back his face was inches from mine. His hand slid over my knee, up my thigh, until his warm hand reached the crotch of my cotton panties.

"Larissa? Is that your name?" he whispered in my ear, as his fingers gripped the seam of my panties and yanked down, the wetness leaving a trail on my leg before he flung them aside.

"Yes," I breathed, as his mouth closed over my collarbone and the car began to move forward.

"I've been waiting for this all day," he said, before his lips crushed mine in a kiss that was tender and assertive all at once.

I could feel his hard length against my hip as he pulled me onto his lap and slipped his hand between my legs. A shudder passed through me as his fingers slid between my wet folds and inside me.

"I knew as soon as Jessica showed me your picture that I had to have you," he whispered, as his tongue flicked in and out of my ear.

I could feel myself becoming engorged with pleasure as he slid his fingers out of me and gently stroked my clit using my own nectar.

I can't believe I'm about to have sex with Chase Underwood! And I'm getting paid for it!

My pelvis writhed and grinded against his touch as his lips explored the curve of my jaw. My limbs filled with so much pleasure my entire body quaked. He kissed my throat and tickled my nub until my body released a final shudder. I fell limp against the leather seat and he sat upright looking very pleased with himself. He lifted my black panties off the floor of the car and held them out to me. My arm wobbled as I reached for them, but he pulled them back at the last second and held them to his nose.

"Mmm... Like an autumn pear," he said with a grin then he handed them over. They were soaked with my juices so I stuffed them into my purse. "Where do you live?"

That's it? For $5,000?

Jessica specifically told me I wasn't allowed to give clients my home address and definitely was not supposed to go home with them, for safety purposes. I wasn't sure if these rules applied to Chase Underwood so I decided to take a chance. He was either so dissatisfied with me he wanted to get me out of his car or the night wasn't over yet. I was hoping it was the latter.

"355 Warren... apartment 4," I breathed, as I attempted to sit upright and check my hair in my hand mirror.

My hands shook as I steadied the mirror in my hands. It had been months since I'd been touched like that by anyone other than myself. Hanging out with Shane for two years had not done wonders for my sex life. I had to lie about this to Jessica during my interview. I actually told her I had been in an open sexual relationship up until last month. Shane gave me pointers on what to say.

I could feel Chase staring at me as I slipped the mirror into my purse. My stomach was in knots wondering whether I had blown this, my only chance to conquer my ever-growing mountain of school loans and credit-card debt. My only chance to get fucked by a man—a hot, powerful man—in almost six months.

The car pulled up beside the curb of 355 Warren, a Spanish-style apartment building on the exterior; tiny artists' lofts with high ceilings on the interior. I waited for him to say something, to ask to come inside, but he stared at me with an unreadable expression in his dark eyes.

"You can go now," he said, nodding toward the car door.

You can go now? That's it.

I glanced down at his crotch as I reached for the door handle behind me. His bulging erection threatened to break through his trousers. I wanted to bend over and take him into my mouth, but he was telling me to leave. *Mixed messages?* No, I definitely screwed this one up. I'd have to start packing my bags to leave L.A. in the morning.

2

A sudden bouncing on my bed woke me and I opened my eyes to find Shane sitting next to me in his boxers with a gleeful expression of triumph lighting up his gorgeous face. Oh, the things I would do to him if he didn't find girls completely *meh*.

"So… how did it go?" he asked.

I sighed as I sat up and adjusted my ponytail. "I don't know," I mutter. "He rubbed my—you know—until I came then he basically kicked me out of his car."

I couldn't say the names of female body parts around Shane. It was too much for him. Every month, when I got my period, he basically holed himself up in the café down the street for four days.

"He just kicked you out onto the street?"

I debated whether I should tell him that Chase dropped me off at the apartment. I still hadn't divulged his identity to Shane.

"Okay, you can't tell anybody, but the client… it was Chase Underwood."

"I know," Shane gloated. "I did a little digging around while you were gone."

I rubbed my eyes as I shook my head. "Shane, you can't tell anyone, especially Jessica, but I let him drop me off here last night. I mean, how the fuck was I supposed to say no to Chase Underwood?"

Shane's hands covered his cheeks as he stared at me in amazement. "Oh, honey, you just hit the jackpot."

"What? Did you not hear what I just said? I spent, like, two seconds with him before dropped me off at home—and I didn't even have sex with him."

"Larissa, if he made you come then dropped you off at home, the man is coming back for more. Besides, I heard he was browsing Jessica's catalogue for months before he settled on you. I heard Mr. Senator and his wife have *never even had sex!* The marriage is some kind of business agreement between them to further his career."

"I don't buy it. There is no way you would know this," I said, as I sprung out of bed and made my way across the gleaming beech floors toward the bathroom.

A knock at the door made me stub my toe on the ottoman. I looked to Shane to see if he was expecting someone. His eyes were wide as we stared at each other, both thinking the same thing.

"Answer the door!" I whispered.

He glanced down at his boxers. "I can't answer the door like this."

"Put on your robe!"

"No! You put on your robe. I'm getting dressed," Shane whispered furiously as he pulled on yesterday's T-shirt and jeans.

I reached into the bathroom and pulled my bathrobe off the hook on the back of the door. I wrapped myself in the robe and breathed the fruity scent of my shampoo on the collar. Shane beat me to the front door, now fully dressed.

"Good luck!" he whispered, before he opened the door.

Chase appeared confused for only a split second before he extended his hand to Shane. "Good morning," he said, and I suddenly realized that I never heard him use his smarmy politician voice last night. "I'm here for Miss Larissa Jacobs."

Shane stared dumbstruck as he shook Chase's hand. I stepped forward so he would release the senator.

"Senator Underwood. This is my roommate," I said, as I sidled up next to Shane and pulled his arm away from Chase. "Shane, weren't you just leaving?"

Chase's shoulders seemed to relax at this new information, but Shane still couldn't speak.

I pushed him out the door. "Go get me a coffee," I ordered him. "But don't rush!"

Shane crossed the walkway and descended the steps to the courtyard in a daze. I turned to Chase and my heart pounded wildly as he smiled at me with those perfect lips and teeth.

"Can I come in?" he asked, his politician voice gone again, replaced by the suave voice that I remembered from last night.

"Of course," I said, stepping aside so he could enter our domain.

It was a mess. Shane must have had company the day before. My unmade bed stood empty in the corner a few feet away from Shane's unmade bed.

"Nice," he remarked, as I closed the front door.

As soon as I turned around, he was there. His fingers trailed down the side of my face before he brushed aside a few strands of hair. I froze as my nipples hardened beneath my robe. He pulled the waist-tie on my robe and his hands slid over my shoulders and down arms until the robe fell into a pile at my feet.

"Put your hands up," he commanded. I obliged as he held both my wrists in one hand and leaned in to whisper in my ear. "Do you know why I'm here?"

His free hand slid under the waistband of my panties and traveled down until it was on me again, so warm and electric.

I moaned. "I think I have an idea."

His mouth fell over mine, his tongue exploring the crease of my lips before he pushed inside and my body arched. His fingers slid inside me and unearthed my wetness, using it to glide his thumb in circles over my hard nub.

His mouth moved to my jaw then the sensitive spot where my neck met my shoulder. "I'm here to teach you a lesson," he whispered. "Never give your address to strangers." He lifted me into his arms and carried me to my bed. He threw me down on the mattress and tore off his jacket. "Take off your clothes."

I hastily yanked off my T-shirt and panties as my slit ached to be filled with him. He grinned as he undressed before me revealing a body so well sculpted it wasn't possible his wife could resist this. He slid a condom over his long erection and crawled across the bed toward me. He wrapped his hands around my waist as I we stood on our knees facing each other. His erection grazed my pelvis as he leaned in and sunk his teeth into my shoulder.

His hands stroked my breasts, squeezed my nipples, caressed my ribs, and moved down my back until he gripped my backside in his strong hands and lifted me. I wrapped my legs around his waist and gasped as he entered me.

I gripped tightly to his neck as we bucked against each other, the warm friction of his pelvis against my sensitive clit sending me skyrocketing toward ecstasy. I threw my head back and he licked the hollow of my neck as he drove deep into me. He quickly lifted me off his lap and set me down on the bed so I lay before him waiting to be ravaged.

He straddled my waist and I cupped my breasts together, ready to receive him. He slid his erection between my breasts and thrust his hips back and forth, slow at first then building speed. The head of his hard member was an inch from my mouth as he thrust his hips toward me. I released my breasts and placed my hand on the base of his cock.

He moved forward, closer to my face, and moaned with pleasure as I covered my teeth with my lips and took him into my mouth. His fingers ran through my hair to the back of my head to support my head as he rocked gently back and forth. My juices accumulated between my legs as his cock prodded the back of my throat.

He reached behind his back and caressed my clit as he thrust himself into my mouth. My legs quivered with the pleasure building inside me. He thrust a few more times, nice and slow, and my eyes watered as we both climaxed at once.

His cock slid out of my mouth and he collapsed next to me on the bed. "That was fucking amazing," he said, his voice husky with exhaustion.

I flipped onto my stomach and raked my fingers down his rock hard chest. "Let's do it again."

He chuckled. "On one condition."

My hand skated down his abdomen, over his new erection, and began massaging his balls. His eyes rolled back with ecstasy as I rolled my fingers slowly and gently over his sac.

"What condition?" I whispered in his ear as his hand clasped my bottom and slid between my cheeks, sending shivers through me as he gently stroked my crease.

"You let me take you to dinner tonight," he replied, letting out a soft moan as my tongue explored the soft curves of his ear.

I wanted to ask if I would be on the clock. I desperately needed the income, but another part of me didn't want the money. I wanted to have dinner with him without the price tag floating over our heads. I knew it shouldn't matter, but I also wanted to find out if what Shane said about his wife was true.

I climbed on top of him and arched my back as he entered me. "Yes," I breathed as his fingers slid between my folds to find my nub. "I'll have dinner with you, Mr. Senator."

His thrusts lifted me off the bed as his fingers guided me quickly into the throes of another orgasm. "Call me Chase."

3

"You can't wear that," Shane said, vetoing my sixth outfit.
"What's wrong with this one?" I whined, holding out my arms to get a better look at my turquoise-blue strapless dress and silver heels in the mirror.

Shane shook his head, which rested in his boyfriend's lap. Shane's boyfriend, Jackson Kim, was almost as gorgeous as Shane, but his attitude could be a bit prickly.

"What do you think, Jack?" I asked, spinning around so the skirt of my dress fluttered around me.

"Somebody get Kate Hudson on the phone 'cause you look like bad chick-flick waiting to happen," Jack replied, as he lifted Shane's head off his lap so he could stand from the bed. "Let me help you."

I tried to pay attention to Jack's advice as he tossed dress after dress out of the shared walk-in closet and onto the floor, but all I could think of was Chase. Where was he taking me? It had to be somewhere no one would recognize him, but places like that didn't exist for Chase Underwood. He had to be taking me somewhere private. *His house?* No, the Democratic senator from California didn't live in L.A. He lived in the hills of San Diego. I remembered watching that on a nightly news special a few weeks ago.

What am I doing?

He's running for president. Wasn't that how Marilyn Monroe got herself killed, involving herself with the Kennedys? Oh, great. Now my thoughts were starting to sound like those of a conspiracy nut. This was a bad idea. I had to call him to cancel. If Jessica found out I agreed to go out to dinner with him without telling him to book it through the service I'd probably be fired on the spot.

But... I didn't have Chase's phone number. There was no backing out now and part of me was bubbly with glee over it.

I kept thinking of his hands, so soft yet strong, lifting me and positioning me so his cock was at just the right angle. I was getting hot just thinking of it.

"I'll be right back," I said to Jack, as he began rummaging through my skirts.

I scampered to the bathroom and locked the door behind me. I lowered the lid over the toilet and placed one foot on the lid. As I imagined Chase's tongue on me, my fingers grazed the sensitive skin of my inner thigh and worked their way up. I drew tight circles over my clit as I imagined Chase ravaging me with his mouth, licking and sucking until... Oh, my god. I was fantasizing about the future president giving me head. This was bad.

I felt like a teenager waiting for my boyfriend to pick me up to go the movies. Chase asked me to stand in front of the apartment building to wait for him. I crossed and uncrossed my arms a million times in the ten minutes I waited on the sidewalk. When the black car pulled up in front of me, the door didn't open automatically as it had outside the hotel last night.

Across the street, a young guy at a bus stop watched me as I approached the car. I quickly opened the door, just a crack, and slipped inside.

His brown hair was not combed in the usual politician's clean-cut coif. Tonight, his hair was a little messier, in a sexy way, and he wore a gray sport coat over a white polo and black jeans. It was definitely designer clothes, probably tailored just for his exquisite body, but the casual attire still put me at ease.

"You look beautiful," he remarked, as his driver whisked us away in our black chariot.

"Thanks," I muttered, trying not to look down at the outfit Jack put together for me. It screamed *young, carefree wife of a politician;* exactly the look Jack insisted I should be going for. "Where are we going?"

He smiled, that dazzling politician smile, and my stomach vaulted. "It's a surprise, but I'll give you a hint," he said, as he reached across the distance between us and ran his finger softly over the edge of my ear. "I've never taken anyone there."

A shiver passed over my skin as his fingers slithered down my neck before he pulled his hand away. I wanted to believe that he saw something in me that prompted him to choose me over the other seventeen girls working for Jessica; a beautiful quality I had yet to glimpse in myself. But the cynical part of my brain was telling me to run away from this man before he destroyed me the way he had supposedly helped destroy the American economy.

The twenty-three-minute ride from our apartment toward Malibu went from grungy to breathtaking as we drove along the cliffs on Pacific Coast Highway overlooking the Pacific Ocean.

I glanced at him every few minutes to find him staring at me, taking in every inch of me.

I still didn't know if I was being paid for this excursion, and the astronomical balance on my student loans kept flashing in my mind. I wanted to ask him if this was a real date, but I didn't have the guts to question the future President of the United States.

The car pulled into the parking lot of a deserted restaurant propped on the edge of a cliff. Even the view from the parking lot was spectacular as the sun set over the Pacific.

"Is this place closed?" I asked, as I glanced around the empty lot.

A smile curled the corner of his mouth. "This is my restaurant. I closed it down so we could have dinner in private. You're not allergic to seafood, are you?"

I shook my head unable to speak. Chase and I would be alone in his restaurant; a restaurant with a gorgeous view. I felt an intense desire to pinch myself.

"Come," he said, as he exited the car.

I had to keep myself from thinking stupid things like *I wish he would hold my hand* as we walked toward the restaurant. When we reached the tall, mahogany-framed glass doors, he pulled a single key out the pocket of his sport coat and slid it into the keyhole. He held the door open for me and the smell of grilled seafood and fried garlic made my mouth water.

A man in a black shirt and slacks appeared at my right. "Your coats?" he said, and I hastily removed the ivory blazer Jack picked out for me, but Chase kept his coat on.

He kept his hand on the small of my back as he guided me toward a glass door leading to an outdoor dining area. As soon as we took our seats in our cushioned chairs at the table with the best view of the ocean, another man in black appeared with two glasses of ice. He poured sparkling water over the ice and scuttled away before I could even thank him.

"You're wondering whether you're being paid for this," Chase finally spoke to my worried thoughts.

"What? Of course, not," I insisted, though the lie felt sticky in my throat.

"Don't lie to me, Larissa," he said, and I suddenly felt as if I was eight years old again, being chastised by my father for setting my pet turtle free in the neighbor's garden. "If we are going to come to an agreement about our arrangement, you cannot lie to me."

Our arrangement?

"I'm sorry. I don't understand what you mean."

The waiter returned before Chase could clarify.

"We'll both have the seared Yellowfin. And bring a fruit basket, please," he rattled off our order to the waiter without consulting me, and with such politeness; it was extremely hot.

When the glass door closed softly behind the waiter, Chase smiled. "I'm prepared to offer you a position in my campaign."

I thought I knew what type of position, or rather positions, he was going to offer me, but I couldn't afford to pay off my student loans and my rent on an intern's wages.

I shook my head. "I can't afford to work on your campaign. That's why I took the job at *Black Tie*. I'm sorry."

CASSIA LEO

The waiter materialized again with a tray covered in bowls of fresh cut pineapple, watermelon, strawberries, and raspberries. He set the bowls in the center of the table and turned to leave.

Chase grabbed his arm and the man looked alarmed. "We are not to be bothered until our food is ready. Is that understood?" The man nodded quickly before he scurried back into the restaurant. "I think I can make it worth your while," Chase continued as he stood from his chair.

He plucked a strawberry from the bowl and took a bite out of the luscious fruit. He savored it for a moment before he swallowed. He leaned over me and his lips fell softly over mine. The taste of strawberry on his tongue made my stomach flutter as he cupped my face in his hands.

"Stand up."

I obeyed his command immediately, the feet of my chair squealing as he kicked it across the tiled floor. He slunk behind me, running his hand down my arm as his lips grazed my neck.

I began to panic. What was he doing and how long would it take? How much longer did we have before our meals were ready and the waiter returned?

"I'll pay off your debts, you'll get a company car, and I can offer you..." he whispered a number in my ear that nearly made my heart stop. "Is that sufficient, Larissa?"

His hands slid down my waist and over my hips. He tugged the skirt of my dress up and I had a moment of panic as his hand glided up my thigh.

"No panties?" he remarked. "I like that."

Jack was the one who suggested no panties. That was the "carefree" part of the outfit.

Chase's right hand slid between my cheeks as his left hand reached for a folded napkin on the table. "Put your hands behind your back," he whispered. I obliged and he immediately tied the napkin around my wrists. "What is your answer, Miss Jacobs?" He turned me around so I was facing him then he grasped both my arms and forced me to sit in my chair. "Just relax."

He knelt down on one knee and propped my legs on his shoulders as his tongue explored my slick nether regions. The pleasure burst through my center all the way to my limbs and I tossed my head back. His finger curled inside me, stroking my spot as his tongue caressed my bud with increased urgency. My hips bucked uncontrollably as he brought me to the brink of orgasm and stopped.

4

"What's wrong?" I asked breathily.

He raised his eyebrows. "What is your answer? Can I welcome you to the campaign?"

"Oh, god!" I thought, as I pulsated with a need for him to finish me off. This wasn't fair.

Then I considered his offer. With my debts paid off and the salary he was offering, plus the car, I wouldn't have to worry about whether or not this director thought I was ten pounds overweight or that casting director thought my face was not symmetrical enough. So much of my daily worries would disappear with a single word. Then there was the issue of his wife. Would she know? Did she already know?

"I don't know," I said before his blue eyes could sway me toward a premature *yes.*

He smiled as stood up and untied the napkin around my wrists and helped me push in my chair just before the waiter arrived. My insides were aching to have him inside me, but we would have to wait.

The waiter placed two plates laden with steaming seared tuna and vibrant grilled vegetables. The smell was intoxicating.

"Dig in. You're going to need your strength for when I attempt to convince you later."

I gobbled up my food as fast as I could without making a mess or looking like a complete pig. When I was done, I patted my mouth with my napkin and took a sip of water, nearly spilling the drink on myself as something prodded its way between my legs. I looked at Chase and his expression was intense as I realized it was his foot fondling me.

"Are you ready?" he asked and I nodded frantically. "Good. Stand up."

As I stood from the table, he also stood and swiped all the plates off the table, sending a bowl of raspberries careening off the side of the cliff to the rocks below. My heart raced as he glided across the distance between us. He grasped my arms and turned me so I faced the now barren tabletop.

He pulled my dress up and over my head and tossed it to onto the tiled floor. I felt completely exposed worrying if our waiter or the kitchen staff were watching from beyond the tinted glass wall separating us from the interior dining space.

"Bend over," he ordered me, and I did as he pleased.

My breasts pressed against the cool glass tabletop as he leaned against me, his weight pressing my belly against the glass as his tongue explored the folds of my ear. He entered me as he bit down on my shoulder and I gasped loudly.

"You are going to accept," he grunted, his arm wrapped around my waist. He pulled me closer so he could enter me even deeper. "Aren't you?"

His other hand reached around and caressed my clit, alternating between a soft and urgent touch. I screamed with pleasure and my cries echoed over the cliffs. My body quaked, my legs turning to jelly, as he brought me to orgasm, but he wasn't finished.

He pulled out of me and continued to rub my bud as he aimed to make me come again. I was almost there when his finger slid back and eased between my ass cheeks. He massaged and stroked gently until his thumb slid into the hole and I panted with bliss. He pulled out his finger and my juices guided him into the place no man had ever gone.

"Oh, my god!" I screamed. "Yes!"

He licked my neck as he pounded into me. "Is that 'yes' for me?"

The table shook beneath us as he stabbed me over and over again. The warm sensation of an inevitable orgasm spread through me.

"Fuck, yes," I breathed. "Don't stop."

His warmth filled me as he came inside me and collapsed on top of my back. My breasts squeaked against the glass tabletop as he kissed my neck while he was still inside me.

Does he want to go again? I'm going to be so sore tomorrow.

Just as this thought crossed my mind, he pulled out. I turned to face him, feeling utterly exposed with the ocean breeze accentuating the wetness on my neck and between my legs.

"I'll take you home so you can pack a bag. We're hitting the trail tomorrow," he said, as he zipped up his pants and tucked his polo back into his jeans. He picked up my dress and handed it to me.

"What about your wife?" I asked. I had to ask. If I was going to accompany him on the campaign trail I had to know if I was risking having my name and dress size plastered across the covers of tabloid magazines.

His eyes bore into me, probably trying to figure out the sub-text beneath my question. "My wife and I haven't so much as breathed on each other the entire time we've been married. My wife has been in love with another man since before she even met me, rather, before she was hired by my campaign manager."

I began to wonder why such a handsome, powerful man had to hire a wife and an escort. Then I realized it probably had to do with the fact that you can buy silence. Is that what he wanted me for: my silence?

"Don't let all those questions brewing inside your mind stand in the way of the opportunity of a lifetime," he said, as he leaned in and planted a soft kiss on the corner of my mouth. "I'm not going to be the president forever."

CHASE
PART II: DISCLOSURE

1

Carrying on a secret affair with the most wanted politician in America was tricky at best. At it's worst, my affair with presidential candidate Chase Underwood would be a racing nightmare of primping and prepping for one publicity event after another. At it's best, our affair was the naughtiest, most pleasurable relationship I'd ever been in.

Relationship.

Chase's word, not mine. The word was plastered all over the nondisclosure agreement he had presented to me last night, right after giving me multiple orgasms with his talented tongue.

"That's not fair," I had said, as he insisted I read aloud sections fifteen through nineteen while he lightly kissed every inch of my body. "'Number fifteen: Recipient shall submit to Candidate's requests, whether related to the Campaign or sexual in nature, in a timely manner; preferably, as soon as such request is made.'" I paused and reread the sentence to myself to make sure I had read it correctly. "What is this?" I asked, as he kissed the inside of my knee.

The hotel lamp cast a soft, golden glow over his brown hair and reflected brilliantly off the few gray hairs he refused to dye.

"I just want to make sure we're clear on the terms of this relationship," he said, his lips moving lightly over my knee to the top of my thigh. "Keep reading."

He slid his hand over my abdomen until he reached my breast. My back arched as my fingers clenched tightly around the sheets of our hotel bed and the contract in my other hand.

I swallowed my pleasure and continued. "'Number sixteen: Recipient shall submit to regular mental, physical, and dental health examinations. Recipient shall also maintain her physical and mental health through regular exercise, healthy diet, therapeutic spa treatments, and, if necessary, regular sessions with a clinical therapist.'" I stopped reading and Chase chuckled, as if he knew what I was about to say. "Therapy?"

"Come now, Larissa. I see a therapist. I'm not implying you need one, but it gets pretty stressful when the campaign is running at full tilt. I want you to know that if you need to talk to anyone, other than me, I can provide that. All my staffers get full health benefits."

"Of course, they do. What would the press think if you didn't provide your employees health care when you're out there stumping for single payer?"

"You've been doing your homework." He kissed my hipbone, sending a shiver through me that stiffened my nipples. "Keep reading. I love listening to your voice."

"'Number seventeen: Recipient shall address Candidate respectfully at all times, in public as 'Sir' and in private as 'Sir' or 'Mr. President'.'" My mouth went slack with shock. "In *private*? Are you kidding?"

His tongue traced a ring around my nipple and the cool air in the hotel room made my entire body shiver.

"Say it."

"No."

"Larissa." His erection grazed my thigh as he slithered up and kissed my collarbone. "You're being a very bad girl."

"Don't you mean I'm being a very bad recipient?"

"Don't make me bring out my paddle."

Something about this sentence threw me over the edge. "Put it in," I murmured.

"What's the magic word?"

"Put it in, please... Mr. President."

He slid into me and I moaned as I tossed the contract to the floor.

"Say it again."

"Mr. President," I said, relishing the feel of the word on my tongue as I wrapped my legs around his waist. "Faster, please, Mr. President."

The air inside the private jet was too warm and smelled too strongly of leather and French roast coffee. Three days spent with Chase and I already knew his favorite brand of coffee, his shoe size, and the password to his Facebook profile. He gave me a long list of his internet passwords, which I would be using to check his emails, Tweet for him, and post status updates on his behalf. I had gone from rookie escort to Senior Personal Assistant to the future president of the United States in less than a week.

I kept going over the five extra clauses tacked onto my non-disclosure agreement in my head and wondering what I'd gotten myself into. The last clause in the NDA was obviously the most important.

19. Recipient agrees all aspects of her relationship with Candidate, whether related to Campaign or sexual in nature, must be kept confidential, unless Agreement is declared null and void by Candidate. In the event of the Candidate's untimely death, Recipient shall remain bound by this Agreement for not less than seven years.

Chase came back to our cabin after his chat with the pilot, adjusting his tie and looking very pleased with himself. "The pilot says we have nothing but clear skies ahead of us. Maryland, here we come."

He sat in the seat next to me and immediately pulled out his iPhone to check his emails.

"I can do that," I said, pulling out the new iPhone he purchased for me two days ago.

He smiled at me as he tucked his phone into his coat pocket and leaned toward me. "You can do that…?"

"I can do that, Sir," I murmured, as he kissed the corner of my mouth.

He planted a soft kiss on the tip of my nose and sat back. "Fasten your seat belt, Larissa. I'm a strong believer in the old adage safety first."

I'll bet you are. After all, that was the whole point of the NDA, wasn't it?

My heart hammered as the plane roared down the runway. I hated airplanes. As soon as we were at cruising height, Chase removed his seat belt then reached over and undid mine.

"Come with me."

I followed him through a locked door toward the rear of the plane. We passed through a cabin where twelve staffers sat in equally luxurious accommodations.

As we passed, Chase squeezed the shoulder of a young fellow with curly hair hunched over a computer. "Don't work so hard, Isa. Relax a little or you'll scare off the young ladies."

Isa grinned sheepishly. "Just checking the latest polls, Sir."

"Larissa, this is Heather Rodin," Chase said, as we came to the back of the cabin where a mousy girl was busy typing a message into her phone. "Heather works for the *Times*. She's doing a feature on my visit to Maryland. I told her she could speak to you tomorrow, after you've become more acquainted with my staff and the campaign. I thought you two should meet before we land and they whisk us all off to separate hotel rooms."

Heather cocked her eyebrow as she held out her hand to me. Her hand was tiny and a bit clammy. "Nice to meet you, Larissa. I look forward to speaking with the newest, *closest* member of Chase's campaign."

"Likewise. Pleasure meeting you, Heather. By the way, I love your shoes. I have a pair just like those in the nude color. Had to leave them at home to conserve space in my luggage. You have great taste."

Heather smirked at my compliment as I turned to follow Chase back to our private cabin. As soon as he closed and locked the door he cast a sly grin in my direction.

"Very smooth complimenting the reporter. Thank you."

"Thank my acting coach."

"I already did thank your acting coach."

"Shut up!" I said, playfully punching him in the arm.

He laughed as he took a seat on the leather sofa and began loosening his tie. "Truth be told, Heather is something of a thorn in my side. She contacted my publicist yesterday at the last minute and we couldn't really say no after that big speech about transparency last week."

I took a seat next to him and reached across to help him with his tie. "She seems a bit nosy and suspicious, if you ask me. I mean, what makes her think I'm the closest member of your campaign? I think Teddy qualifies for that position."

Teddy Holt was Chase's bullish campaign manager, known for making staffers weep with his quick abrasive wit and impossible deadlines. He was already in Maryland waiting for us. Just the thought of meeting him today made me want to cry.

Chase pulled me onto his lap as I slipped his tie off. "Right now, I think you're much more qualified for that position."

He kissed me hard as he clutched my hair, which was newly cut and dyed at Chase's request.

"Are you wearing panties?"

"No, Sir."

"Good girl," he replied, as he slid me off his lap. "Now bend over so I can show you what will happen if I ever catch you wearing panties with a skirt."

18. Recipient shall be subject to occasional light physical punishment from Candidate. Punishment will be issued with Recipient's safety in mind and may include, but is not limited to, spanking, whipping, choking, and application of physical restraints. Should such punishment become too much for Recipient to handle, Recipient agrees to use safe words. Recipient will use the safe word "yellow" when punishment should slow down or ease up. Recipient will use the word "red" when punishment should stop immediately.

I bent over the sofa with my feet planted firmly on the floor. He yanked my skirt up, exposing my cheeks. The first two spankings were light and I could feel my lips becoming slick with my juices. The third smack stung quite a bit.

"More?"

"Yes, Sir."

"Later," he said, as he bent over me and kissed the sensitive spot behind my ear. He turned me around so I fell back onto the sofa then he spread my legs and gazed at me hungrily. "Now it's time to reward you for being such a fast learner."

2

The flight landed in Maryland ahead of schedule, which gave me less time than I wanted to fix my hair and makeup after my romp with Chase. The ride to the hotel was awkward. His driver, George, had to take a later flight out of L.A. due to personal issues. We had to take a government-issued motorcade to the hotel, which had to be swept for explosives four times. Inside the car, we had to keep our interactions strictly business.

I kept glancing across the leather seat of the limousine at his perfectly shined shoes, his soft manicured hands, his strong shoulders, and that freshly shaven chiseled face. I wanted to tell him how hot he looked. I wanted him to tell me how beautiful I looked. I never felt more beautiful.

From the stylish haircut and mani-pedi to the expensive designer clothes Chase's stylist handpicked for me, I looked like a different person. I looked like the person I had always dreamed of becoming since I left Florida to make it in Hollywood. I should be ecstatic, but something felt off and I knew exactly what it was.

Mrs. Katherine Underwood.

Chase's wife was still his wife and, even if Chase and my old roommate (and the tabloids) claimed they had never been intimate together, I found this hard to believe when I looked at pictures of them kissing on the lips and holding hands. Maybe Chase was just a better actor than I was, but I couldn't imagine pretending to be in love with someone.

"Katherine will be flying in tomorrow," Chase said, breaking the silence in the limo and delivering a painful jolt to my heart. "Please set up a reminder to have George pick her up at the airstrip at 10:30."

I slipped my phone out of my purse and punched in the reminder. "Done."

He could have told me this in the airplane when there wasn't a ten-ton elephant named Katherine sitting between us. He probably only mentioned it now to keep up appearances with the stranger driving the car.

The Secret Service agent opened the door for me and I was immediately taken with how handsome he appeared in his crisp suit and dark sunglasses. As I exited the limo, I brushed past him and caught a whiff of his clean aftershave. Maybe I should just give up on Chase and go for someone more in my league, someone not destined to break my heart.

The hotel was one of the newer, more understated and modern hotels in the center of Baltimore. Chase refused to stay in places like the Four Seasons because he didn't want to be seen as stodgy or pretentious. The sparkle of the glass revolving doors made me dizzy.

As his new assistant, I had to pick up Chase's room keys, make sure his baggage was delivered to the room, and tip the bellhop very well. All this had to be done while Chase raced to a meeting with the mayor of Baltimore to discuss arrangements for tomorrow's rally.

"Let's take my luggage to my room first," I told the bellhop as we entered the elevator. "We'll deliver Ch—we'll deliver the senator's bags after that."

Someone jammed her arm through the elevator doors just as they were about to close. Heather Rodin entered the cabin and pressed the button for the fifth floor.

"Oh, hi, Larissa," she said, feigning surprise at finding me in the same elevator. "A lot of luggage you've got there."

I smiled at her thinly disguised attempt to rattle me. "The senator is in a meeting with Mayor Johnson. Just doing my duty and making sure his luggage arrives in his room."

"Your duty." She pursed her lips as she glanced at my hair then she reached up and smoothed down a piece of my hair. "I always come out of airplanes with my hair in disarray. Did you cut your hair recently? I'm looking for a new stylist and I love this new look of yours."

New look? How did she know this was a new look for me?

I tried to regulate my breathing, but my heart was beating too quickly.

"Sorry. I don't know the name of the stylist. Senator Underwood's personal stylist made the appointment for me. I merely showed up and sat my butt in the chair."

A victorious smile tugged at one corner of her lips as I nervously blurted this reply. The elevator stopped at the fifth floor and she turned to me. "Relax, Larissa. The campaign's only going to get more intense from here on out."

She exited the elevator and disappeared down the corridor as the elevator doors closed. I glanced at the bellhop, who could surely sense the tension, but he was staring at the flashing floor numbers above the doors.

Why were elevator rides with strangers so awkward? So you had to stand next to a stranger for a few seconds in a confined space. Did we really need to completely avoid eye contact?

"She's a reporter," I said, breaking the silence as the elevator climbed toward the seventeenth floor.

"Yeah, I got the academic vibe from the awful shoes she was wearing," he replied with a grin and I laughed as I thought about how I'd lied when I told her I owned the same pair in a different color.

I would have to tip William the bellhop extra for helping me loosen up a little. After we delivered my luggage to my room, we got back in the elevator to head for the penthouse. The elevator doors opened and I couldn't believe my eyes.

The penthouse looked like an ultra-swanky apartment that would be featured in *Modern Home* magazine with a gleaming kitchen, a floating staircase, and a wall of windows that showed off a mind-blowing view of the Atlantic Ocean. I stepped inside and my eyes widened at the sight of the waterfall that seemed to come out of the wall and disappeared into the floor. My heels clicked against the concrete flooring.

William rolled the luggage trolley into the room and began unloading the luggage as I gravitated toward the view. Most of what I saw from this vantage point was rooftops and traffic jams, but somewhere out there inside one of those buildings Chase was shaking hands with the mayor and discussing things no doubt beyond my pay grade. I glanced to my left and saw a bed clothed in sumptuous white linens and suspended above the floor by steel cables. Would Chase and Katherine be sleeping there tomorrow night?

"Ahem. Miss Jacobs."

I shook off this dreary thought and joined William near the elevator door where I handed him two hundred-dollar bills from the wad of cash Chase gave me for "incidentals". Suddenly, I was beginning to feel more and more like a prostitute.

The elevator door opened and William scurried inside as if he were afraid I would discover I'd given him too much money. "Are you going down, Miss?"

I stared at him for a moment as he held the door for me. "Oh, yes, of course. Seventeenth floor."

My phone vibrated as I entered my room. It was a text message from Chase.

Chase:
Make dinner reservations for two
at Dillon's Steakhouse for 8 p.m.

I quickly pulled up my reservations app and made the reservation before I responded.

Larissa:
Done… Sir.

I waited four minutes for a thank-you reply that never came. I tucked the phone back into the inner pocket of my blazer and sighed as I collapsed onto the bed. This was going to be a very long three days.

3

After peeling myself off the bed, I spoke to George to arrange for him to pick up Katherine tomorrow morning and called Dillon's to confirm tonight's reservation. Then I called the local television station to make sure Chase's speech had been delivered. My final call was to room service to ask them to deliver some wine and fruit to the penthouse at eleven p.m. I had to at least pretend to be good at my new job.

At seven p.m., after not hearing from Chase all day, I finally decided to take advantage of the whirlpool tub. I laid my phone on the counter in the bathroom and undressed. I turned the water on in the tub and pressed the button to turn on the jets before I climbed in. I dumped the entire bottle of expensive body wash I found on the countertop into the warm running water and closed my eyes as I laid back.

"Such a shame to hide such a gorgeous body under all those bubbles."

I opened my eyes to find Chase sitting on the edge of the tub.

"I thought you had a dinner reservation. Oh, god. Did they not book it? I called to confirm, I swear."

"Settle down, settle down. The reservation is for eight. I have plenty of time to get there from here. Right now, I had to see you." He reached for my face and brushed aside a lock of damp hair. "I missed you today."

"You missed me?" I said. "Does anyone know you're in here?"

"Of course. I told the mayor you and I are regrouping before tomorrow's rally."

"Shouldn't someone else be here to vouch for you? Maybe, Isa or… Heather?"

"Am I not enough for you?"

I stood from the tub and yanked a towel off the rod.

"Larissa, you don't have to worry. No one thinks we're having an affair."

I struggled to secure the towel around me as I climbed out of the tub. "I don't think I can do this. I should just go back to L.A."

He grabbed me around the waist and pulled my back against him. "Larissa, I know what I'm doing. This is not going to fall apart. I promise."

His lips grazed the back of my ear as his hand pressed firm against my belly. The towel fell as he spun me around so our noses were touching. His lips hovered over mine for a moment before he kissed me tenderly.

I was so lost in his kiss I didn't notice him carrying me out of the bathroom. He laid me gently on the bed and I tried not to squirm as his gaze roamed over every hill and crevice of my body. He sat on the edge of the bed and traced his index finger from my ankle up to my hip where he laid his hand. He leaned over and took my nipple into his mouth, sucking gently as his hand glided over my hip toward my crotch.

His fingers slid between my lips, gliding easily through the wetness. His caress was as light as a whisper, just barely bringing me to the brink before he stopped. His lips left a light trail of kisses over my chest and collarbone before they fell softly over my lips.

I placed my hand on the back of his head and pulled him closer to me, kissing him hungrily, and he quickly pulled away.

"Not now, baby. There'll be plenty of time for that when I get back from my dinner with the mayor."

"But I want you so bad," I whispered, as he kissed my forehead, the tip of my nose, my lips, and my belly before he laid his lips over my engorged clit.

"Oh, god," I cried.

He kissed and licked me so softly I had to look down a few times to make sure he was still there. I was about to explode when he finally pulled away.

"You're leaving?" I asked, as he stood up and straightened his tie.

"Go to my room. Make yourself at home. I'll be back in a couple hours." He licked his lips and smiled. "You make a very delicious appetizer, Miss Jacobs. Just wait till you see what I have planned for the main course."

I called down to room service to have them send up the wine and fruit at nine p.m. instead then I took my time getting ready. When I was satisfied with my understated makeup, I dressed up in the black lingerie I'd purchased for myself yesterday with my "incidentals" money. Though it was plenty warm outside in Baltimore in late August, I brought a trench coat for just this occasion. I got dressed in a conservative pantsuit and grabbed a few files out of my briefcase before I draped the trench coat over my arm and made my way to the penthouse.

I tried hard not to glance around the elevator for surveillance cameras. Chase said he knew what he was doing. I had to stop worrying. If we got caught, it would be the end of his career, not mine. In fact, it would probably propel me to some kind of celebrity status, which may actually give me a leg up when trying to secure acting roles.

But I didn't want it to be over.

I checked the time on my phone and noticed a message from Chase.

Chase:
I'll be there in fifteen.
Wait for me in the bedroom.

I tried not to imagine what would be happening in this bed tomorrow night as I laid on the bed that appeared to be suspended in midair. The bed wobbled a bit under my weight as I removed my stuffy pantsuit and tossed it behind the bed. I decided against the trench coat and instead laid myself out on the bed, waiting for him.

The crotch of my panties was already wet with anticipation of his arrival. The coolness of the linen felt good against my skin. I ran my hands over the comforter then my feet. The friction built between my legs as my feet skated across the fabric until I finally slid my hand inside my panties.

I massaged my clit gently, the way Chase had, and I imagined it was his hand on me. I cupped my breast with my other hand and squeezed my nipple, imagining it was his lips tugging on me.

"Oh, Chase," I breathed. "Don't stop."

I feathered my clit with gentle pressure, easing up as soon as I was about to come. I opened my eyes and Chase was standing at the foot of the bed watching me.

"Don't stop," he commanded, and I obeyed.

I continued almost bringing myself to climax then stopping. I turned onto my belly to give him a better view from behind and he stood rapt with attention at the foot of bed, never moving, never making a move to join me, though I could see the bulge of his erection.

Finally, I stood from the bed and grabbed his tie. "I want you to take me all the way there."

He smiled as I sat back on the bed and pulled him toward me by the tie. "What's the magic word?"

"Make me come, please, Mr. President."

He gazed into my eyes for a moment before he hung his head.

"Wrong magic word? Should I have said 'Sir'?" I asked, as I attempted to pull him on top of me, but he resisted.

"No. This is all wrong." He sat up on his knees between my legs.

"Is the lingerie too much?"

He chuckled as he looked me over. "No, it's this whole thing. Having you here the night before Katherine arrives."

My heart dropped into my stomach as I realized I was about to get dumped.

"No, it's not you," he insisted, as he noticed the hurt expression on my face. "It's me. I need…."

"To focus on the campaign. I understand." I sat up, but he grabbed my arm to stop me.

"Please let me finish." He waited a moment before he let go of my arm and continued. "I need to tell you something. I think... I'm falling in love with you."

I closed my eyes for a moment as I processed these words. When I reopened them I expected to find myself back in my hotel room, waking from some crazy dream, but it wasn't a dream. This was my life. The senator of California, and almost certain future president, was falling in love with me.

"Please say something."

I stared at him for a moment, taking in the beautiful curves of his face and the slightly desperate look in his eyes. "I love you. I do."

His smile flashed for an instant before he grabbed my face and his lips crushed mine. The urgency in this kiss was a stark contrast to the way he had kissed me earlier and it made me want him even more.

"I love you," he whispered in my ear as his lips brushed my earlobe. "I want to make love to you."

We hastily undressed each other and stood on our knees on the bed facing each other. He slipped his hands around my waist and a shiver passed through me as he kissed my shoulder.

"You're so beautiful."

"Don't you want to spank me, Mr. President," I murmured, as his lips moved down to my breast. I didn't want to sound too eager, but I couldn't stop thinking of the way he held me so firmly as he swatted my behind. I wanted more and he never finished.

He lightly bit my nipple and I gasped. "Don't worry. I haven't forgotten. There's still plenty more punishment coming to you."

He pushed me back onto the bed and spread my legs open. "But right now, I just want to make you scream with pleasure, no pain." He kissed my clit hard, the way he had kissed my mouth and I damn near came within seconds before he pulled back. "Turn around, baby."

I flipped over and he pulled my hips up so my ass was in the air. He licked my clit gentle now as he slid two fingers inside me. He massaged the sensitive spot inside me until I almost felt as if I were going to pee.

I screamed aloud with pure ecstasy as my body quivered. "Oh, my god! Don't stop! I'm going to come!" I bit down on the blanket as my body released a giant shudder.

Before I could recover, he slid his cock inside me and the sensation of his balls drumming against my sensitive clit sent me quickly into orgasm number two, soon followed by numbers three and four.

4

Chase insisted it would look far worse if I left his hotel room past midnight. He said no one would notice a thing if we both headed down tomorrow morning at the same time after having a meeting in his suite. Everyone expected us to be joined at the hip. So I spent the night sleeping in his arms and in the morning I gazed at him across the kitchen counter as I sipped my coffee while wrapped in his shirt.

The rally went off without a hitch and I couldn't help but stand in awe of the thousands of people cheering him on. Even if I weren't in love with Chase, I believed him. I didn't know if he would bring universal health care and strengthen our economy and education system, but I believed he would try. He was extremely good at what he did.

It suddenly became hard to breathe as I realized he could very well have used that same political charm on me last night. As soon as we climbed into the car he leaned in to kiss me.

I pushed him away. "Were you lying to me last night the same way you were lying to those people right now?"

As soon as we got to the hotel I wouldn't be able to confront him about this. Katherine would be waiting for him and the rest of my trip would probably be spent trying to avoid her the way I used to avoid my creditors.

"About being in love with you? Of course I wasn't lying. Where is this coming from?"

I glared at him across the cabin of the Towncar unable to read his expression. "Are you using me for sex? I mean, I know you're paying me, but I don't want to think there's more to this if there isn't. You don't have to tell me you love me just to make this whole deal easier for me to swallow. I knew what I was getting into. I may not like the arrangement, but I went into it with my eyes open. I would prefer to keep it that way. Please tell me the truth."

He glared right back at me looking very disappointed. "Larissa, I told you last week and I meant it when I said I'm not going to be president forever. The implication is true. I want to be with you long term. What I said last night is true. I am in love with you. But I can understand if this is too much for you. I never expected you to accept my offer."

Our car was quickly approaching the hotel where a horde of reporters, including Heather Rodin, waited out front.

"George, take us around the block one more time," Chase commanded and we sailed right past the gawking reporters.

The Secret Service car followed closely behind us and Chase's phone rang immediately.

"Everything's fine. Don't call back," he shouted into the phone before he hung up and stuffed it back into his pocket.

"That's just it," I began. "I can't stop thinking of our... arrangement as an offer. It feels cheap and dirty. I feel cheap and dirty."

"I wouldn't exactly call you cheap," he replied with a smirk that quickly disappeared when he saw the shock on my face. "It was a joke, Larissa. The reason I love being with you is because I feel like I can be myself with you."

"What about Katherine? Don't you two ever have a decent conversation or laugh at each other's jokes?"

"I told you Katherine is in love with someone else. Always has been."

"How do you two keep up this charade? It must be exhausting. I mean, I've been with you a week and I feel like I'm going insane, second-guessing myself and my future every five minutes."

Our car rounded the corner and he didn't fight the inertia that carried him toward me. He grabbed my hand and I closed my eyes against the swelling tide of emotions flowing through me. I didn't want to cry. I couldn't cry with a dozen reporters waiting to ask Chase if he'd chosen a running mate yet. This was all too much.

He wiped the first tear from my cheek with his thumb then he kissed away the next tear. "I don't believe in God, but every day I thank whatever force, be it the universe, fate, dumb luck, that brought us together." I opened my eyes and he kissed the corner of my lips. "I'll tear up that stupid NDA. I'll do whatever it takes to keep you here. But even if you decide to go back to L.A., I'm not giving up on you."

I tried to swallow the lump in my throat, but my voice still sounded a bit strangled when I spoke. "I'll stay."

"George, take us on a detour. I need twenty minutes," he called toward the pane of tinted glass separating us from the front seat.

He pulled me onto his lap so I straddled him then he unzipped his pants and entered me. I kissed him hard as I slid up and down, his hard cock filling me as his fingers glided over my hard nub. He moaned and I gasped as we bucked faster then slower then faster.

"Harder!" I cried.

He put one hand on each side of my waist to hold me steady as he pounded me from beneath.

"You're so fucking hot," he groaned, as he approached climax.

I quickly slid off him before he could come inside me then I got down on my knees and took him into my mouth.

"Oh, god," he breathed, as his cock hit the back of my throat.

He tasted like the two of us and it made me so hot I grabbed the base of his cock with one hand and used my other hand to pleasure myself. I pulled down on the base of his cock to stretch the skin taut as I licked the tip, savoring the taste and caressing every ridge. I took him into my mouth again and pumped my head back and forth quickly, pushing myself to take him in deeper with every bob of my head. I rubbed the tip of his cock over my lips as if I were applying lipstick then I licked it from tip to base as if it were a Popsicle and he moaned with pleasure.

I took him into my mouth again and didn't stop bobbing until he came into the back of my throat. I swallowed his essence, a slightly bitter, but nonetheless tasty, treat. I cast a sly grin at him as I sat back on the seat.

"Did you finish?" he whispered in my ear and I shook my head. "Then lay back."

His tongue lapped softly at my clit and I clawed the leather seat as my body convulsed. "Oh, yes!" I screamed. "Yes! Yes!"

His arms were locked around my thighs to keep me from squirming as he refused to stop until I came a second time. I collapsed against the seat and he slithered over me until he was on top of me. The weight of him made me feel safe and I breathed a deep sigh.

He kissed the tip of my nose before he rested his forehead against my forehead. "I'm going to do everything I can to make you feel comfortable and secure. I'm going to take care of you. Will you allow me to do that, Miss Jacobs?"

I couldn't help but smile. "Yes, Sir."

I managed to get my hair and makeup looking halfway decent before we arrived at the hotel. Some reporters had left, but at least half were still waiting, including Heather Rodin and two people I had been dreading meeting for days: Teddy Holt and Katherine Underwood.

We stepped out of the car and I immediately switched into assistant mode. "I'll schedule that dinner for you and Kitty Stoddard," I said to Chase, keeping my eyes on him so I wouldn't have to look at the various faces glaring at me. "And I'll schedule the conference call with Mercy Hospital for four p.m. to discuss tomorrow's appearance."

I glanced at Katherine briefly, taking in her perfectly pressed wine-colored suit and plump red lips before I walked briskly toward the hotel entrance. Heather followed me, a few reporters eyeing her suspiciously as she showed no interest in speaking to

Chase. She caught me in the revolving door and squeezed in next to me. I wondered if she could smell the scent of sex on me as the door propelled us into the hotel lobby.

"Can I help you?" I asked, trying my best to keep my voice polite and level.

"What was the hold up? The senator's car passed the hotel twice, but never stopped until now." She held her thumbs over the keyboard on her phone, poised to jot down whatever flub I made.

"It was nothing. He received a phone call then he advised his driver to keep going."

"Really? Was there some kind of threat?"

This girl was not going away.

"I don't know. You'll have to speak with Chase."

She narrowed her eyes at me as we waited for the elevator. "Chase said I had full access to him through you. Are you going to answer my question or do I have to do my own digging?"

I turned on her as the elevator doors slid open. "We were discussing his appointments and he wanted to finish the discussion before we arrived at the hotel and he was attacked by reporters."

I stormed into the elevator and she followed quickly after me. "I guess I'm going up, too. That lie made me feel extra filthy. I think I need a shower."

This was not going well. I couldn't react emotionally to a reporter or I would ruin everything for Chase. I had to befriend her, but how?

"I'm sorry if you feel deceived, Heather, but I assure you Chase has nothing to hide," I replied. "How about you and I get a drink in the lobby in thirty minutes and we can discuss your feature? I just have to make a few appointments first."

"You call him Chase?"

Shit!

"He insists I call him by his first name. You know how important it is to him to appear personable and approachable."

The elevator stopped at the fifth floor and Heather positioned herself on the threshold to keep the doors from closing. "You have an answer for everything. It seems you've picked up the senator's tricks quite quickly.... See you in thirty minutes, Larissa."

She winked at me before she strode away down the corridor. I jumped as my phone vibrated against my breast. I fumbled around for it in the inner pocket of my blazer and nearly dropped it as it vibrated again in my hand.

"Senator Underwood's office. How may I help you?"

"Larissa, it's me." Chase's voice instantly relaxed me and I leaned against the wall of the elevator to collect myself.

"Sorry. I didn't look at the caller ID."

"I saw Heather follow you into the elevator. I just wanted to make sure everything was okay."

"I told her you made George keep driving so we could finish discussing your appointments. She didn't believe me."

The silence on the other end of the line made me nervous.

"Don't worry about her. I'll call her right now."

"I'm meeting her in thirty minutes to discuss the feature."

"I'll tell her you can't make it because you're going to lunch with Teddy and me."

Great. I was ditching one hostile situation for another.

"We're not really going to lunch with Teddy," he continued, as he probably sensed my trepidation. "I'm taking you shopping."

The elevator doors opened on the seventeenth floor and I walked briskly toward my room as if Heather were still trailing me.

"Shopping? But you just took me shopping two days ago. Shouldn't you be meeting with Teddy to discuss tomorrow's visit to the hospital?"

"This is a different kind of shopping," he replied, and I could hear the smile in his voice. "Larissa, I'd like to take you ring shopping, if that's all right with you."

I nearly dropped the phone as I entered my room. "What—what kind of ring?"

"I know I'm not legally available to you right now, but it won't always be that way. I want to take you shopping for an engagement ring. I want you to know I'm serious about keeping you, if you'll have me."

My limbs suddenly became very weak. I had to sit cross-legged on the carpet to keep from collapsing.

"Larissa? Are you there?"

"I'm here."

"I know this isn't really romantic, asking you over the phone, but I promise I'll make that up to you soon if you promise to be my first *real* wife?"

"I... I have to give that some thought."

"I understand."

"I do love you," I blurted. "I just have to make sure I know what I'm getting into."

"Of course. Would you still like to go ring shopping, just to get a feel for what you're getting yourself into?"

I smiled as I realized this could be the most difficult and important decision of my life and he was still able to successfully make light of it. "I'd love to."

CHASE
PART III: EXPOSURE

1

"I now pronounce you husband and wife. You may kiss the bride."

My sniveling broke the hush inside the chapel as I watched Isa kiss his new wife, Nina.

"Sorry," I whispered to the older gentleman on my right as he cast a disapproving look in my direction. "I'm just really happy for them."

I *was* happy for Isa and Nina. Just eight weeks after they were both hired to work on Chase's campaign, they were tying the knot in a swanky chapel in Vegas four days before the election. They were so certain Chase Underwood was going to win the election, they decided to get the wedding over with so they could use their honeymoon as an excuse to celebrate his victory.

As I watched Chase in his dark gray suit embracing Isa and Nina in the aisle, my eyes were drawn to his right: Mrs. Katherine Underwood. She wore an elegant beige sheath dress with tan heels and her dark hair pulled into a neat twist. My gaze fell to my lap where my hands lay clasped over my pink clutch, my left hand still missing the engagement ring I'd picked out with Chase six weeks ago.

I kept going over that day in my mind. Chase had arrived at my hotel room in Baltimore with a jeweler and a suitcase full of rings that each cost more than I made in a year. I didn't know where he had found a discreet and trustworthy jeweler in such a short amount of time; then again, he was a self-made billionaire who was four days away from being the next president of the United States of America. The countless ways he wielded his power never ceased to amaze me.

"Do you prefer round, oval, marquise, or princess cut?" the jeweler asked in a hushed tone, obviously intimidated by Chase and the circumstances of our meeting.

"Princess," Chase replied for me, giving my hand a tiny squeeze. "Only the best for my princess," he continued, as he planted a soft kiss on my cheekbone.

I should have known at that moment I had very little control over the terms of this engagement.

"Larissa, are you alright?"

How embarrassing. The bride was consoling me on *her* wedding day.

"I'm fine," I said, popping out of my seat and throwing my arms around Nina. "I'm just so happy for you guys."

I watched over Nina's shoulder as the Secret Service agent held the door open for Chase and Katherine at the back of the chapel. They were leaving through the rear entrance, probably being whisked away to their suite or to a secret exit where a car would be waiting to carry them off to another private lunch meeting.

"Larissa?"

"Oh, I'm sorry," I said, letting go of Nina as I tried to focus on her beautiful floral crown and flowing dress instead of the expression of pity on her round face. "Go. Go be with your husband. Enjoy the reception."

"You're not coming?"

"I think I'm just going to go back to my room. I hardly slept last night and I have to rest up for tomorrow night's fundraiser."

Her eyes lit up at the mention of the word husband and she quickly set off down the aisle. Isa gazed at me for a moment. He was the only campaign staffer who I was certain knew about Chase and I.

Isa glanced at his new wife as she approached the chapel doors then back at me. "He's a good man," he whispered. "You deserve a *great* one."

I managed to make it back to my hotel room without another emotional breakdown. I slid the cardkey into the reader on the door and the lock clicked. When I pushed the door open, I couldn't believe my eyes.

All the furniture in my hotel room was gone and a trail of rose petals and candles cut a path across the floor toward the balcony. The French doors stood open displaying a breathtaking view, but the lights of Las Vegas couldn't match the radiance of Chase's smile.

As my feet carried me forward, part of me hoped this was it. He was finally going to properly propose and give me the ring I'd been waiting to wear for six weeks. Another part of me thought this wasn't right. In my hotel room, overlooking a city known for legal prostitution with his legal wife somewhere nearby.

But, as I approached the balcony and breathed in the scent of rose petals and fire, I knew there would be no resisting. I crossed the threshold onto the balcony and Chase held out his hand. I placed my hand in his and he softly pressed his lips to my ring finger. His eyes were locked on mine as he gauged my reaction then his lips curled into a smile.

"My mother once told me that where you find love is where you'll find success," he said, as he pulled me toward the waist-high wall enclosing the balcony. "I told her I had to find success before I could think of falling in love."

Chase had never spoken to me about his mother, though from the daily phone calls I gathered they were still quite close.

"My dad told me I would find the man of my dreams the moment I stopped looking," I replied, as we gazed at the shimmering lights of the Vegas strip. "My mom was a little less romantic. She told me I'd find love when I found a guy who didn't mind the way I looked sitting on the throne."

Chase laughed out loud, a robust laugh that rattled my bones. "I'm sure you're quite the vision sitting on the throne," he said, casting me a sly sideways glance. "I like your mom."

"Yeah, well, she doesn't like me very much. I haven't spoken to her since I left home two years ago."

He turned to me and I expected to find pity in his eyes. What I found instead was concern. "Larissa, you have to speak to your mother. She has to know about your success."

You call this success?

"What am I supposed to tell her? I'm working on the most expensive and feverish campaign in the history of the world, oh, and by the way, Mom, I'm having an affair with the soon to be President of the United States."

He looked as if I had just told him he lost the election.

"I'm sorry. That came out wrong."

He shook his head then turned back to the city lights. "No, you're right. You can't tell your mother about your new job. She'll question you and that will just lead to more questions."

Though Chase had kept his word and torn up the non-disclosure agreement he made me sign six weeks ago before I came to work on his campaign, the expectation of silence was more than implied.

I let out a derisive chuckle. "Of course. We have to protect Senator Underwood from the press."

"Larissa, you knew what you were getting into when you came on the road with me."

"Now *you're* the one who's right."

I turned to leave and he grabbed my arm. "Don't go."

I gazed at the trail of rose petals and candles then at his fingers curled firmly around my forearm—the same fingers that were curled inside me last night—and my resolve ebbed.

He pulled me toward him and clasped my face in his hands. "The election is four days away. Can we please just enjoy tonight?"

The cool desert air swept up the tiny hairs on my neck and I shivered as his lips hovered over mine.

"The election maybe four days away, but you're going to be president for four years. I don't know if I can wait that long."

"Maybe I can help you make up your mind."

His lips crushed mine and I gripped his tie so I wouldn't collapse at his feet. Every part of me throbbed with the need for his touch. He lifted my dress over my head and tossed it onto the floor of the balcony. My nipples hardened under the kiss of the frigid breeze. He gently leaned me back over the balcony wall, taking my nipple into his warm mouth, and I was immediately reminded of our rendezvous at his cliff-side restaurant.

His hands lightly caressed my back and cheeks as he licked and sucked my breasts. I gazed at the twinkling stars above us and, against all reason, I made a wish on the first star I saw: *Please let me be strong enough for him.*

His tongue traced a line over the hollow of my neck and he took my face in his hands again. "I love you, Larissa," he whispered. "One day it will be you and me walking down that aisle. I promise."

I reached down to loosen his belt and unzip his trousers. His belt clinked as his pants dropped and I hastily undid his tie and peeled off his blazer and shirt. I ran my fingers over his hard chest and down his abs until I reached his cock. I lightly rubbed my thumb over the slippery head and he moaned. I crouched down and took him into my mouth.

"Jesus Christ," he groaned, as I wrapped one hand around the base of his cock and raked the nails of my other hand over his chest.

I bobbed slowly then swiftly, bringing him to the brink of ecstasy before he slipped his hand beneath my arms and pulled me up. I wrapped my legs around his waist as he lifted me. He fit so perfectly inside me I let out an eager gasp as I clung to him. His teeth dug deeper into my shoulder with every thrust.

I hooked my arm around his neck and clutched onto his rock hard bicep to balance myself. I didn't know how he had the strength to hold me for so long when he was clearly on the verge of losing himself. We rocked rhythmically, grinding against each other, until his body quivered and he came inside me.

He slowly knelt on one knee and placed me down gently so I straddled his leg. He exhaled hot, ragged breaths into my mouth as he kissed me. I wanted to stay like this forever, but I knew that soon he would go up to his penthouse suite where he and his wife would sleep in separate bedrooms—at least, that's what he told me.

He brushed my hair out of my face and kissed my forehead. "I can tell when you're mind is elsewhere," he said. "I have something to ask you."

No, not here, on a balcony in Vegas, in the nude.

He smiled at the hint of panic on my face. "I want you to meet Katherine."

2

I blinked a few times, stunned by his words.

"She wants to meet you," he continued. "And I think it's a good idea to get that out of the way before the election happens and I'll be… unavailable for a while."

I had probably spoken a total of ten words to Katherine Underwood since I joined Chase's campaign six weeks ago. Chase was a master at keeping us apart without raising the suspicions of the press corps that followed him everywhere he went. He even went so far as rescheduling a speaking event at a college so I could be there with him the day after Katherine and Teddy, Chase's campaign manager, left town for a CNN interview. The event coordinator was not pleased when I called him to postpone, but Chase insisted the man would forget all about it once I graced him with my radiant beauty.

"What's your answer, Larissa?" Chase interrupted my thoughts and I gazed at his face as it came back into focus. The chiseled cheekbones and model-perfect lips. And those eyes. A deep-brown that, in the dim lighting, appeared as black as the prospect of meeting Katherine.

"Of course, I'll meet her," I replied. "Will her lover be there?"

Chase wrapped his arm around my waist and pulled me closer to him. He slid his fingers between my wet folds as he kissed my neck and muttered into my skin. "You've already met him."

I let out a small gasp, a mixture of surprise and pleasure, as he gently stroked my clit. "What... oh, god... what do you mean? Who is he?"

He took my earlobe between his teeth and exhaled into my ear. The whoosh of air tickled and made the hairs on my arms stand on end. "Come on, Larissa," he whispered in my ear, as he slid his finger inside me to release more of my wetness. "Don't tell me you can't see that Katherine and Teddy are together."

My body convulsed as he caressed my hard nub in light circles. I let out an involuntary shriek as I climaxed then crumpled against his chest.

"I can't believe it," I said, out of breath and shocked that I had been so completely deceived by Katherine and Teddy's friendship. "But... isn't Teddy your best friend? And... what the hell? Why have you been letting me think we need to keep our relationship a secret from him?"

"I never told you you had to do that, I just assumed it would be best not to confuse things further."

My jaw dropped. "I've been driving myself nuts trying to keep this from Teddy! I was more scared of Teddy reading that feature in the *L.A. Times* than anyone else."

He stood up quickly and began to get dressed. "I don't want to talk about the feature right now."

"Why do you keep doing that? It's coming whether you talk about it or not and there's a good chance Heather Rodin is going to blow the lid on us."

He handed me my dress without looking at me. "I'm going to order some room service. Is Chinese good for you?"

I snatched the dress out of his hand and stomped into the hotel room, kicking up rose petals as I made my way to the bathroom.

"Larissa, stop."

"I want my furniture back!" I shouted, as I stepped over the fat candles.

"I said stop!"

I stopped just outside the bathroom and turned toward him. His face was furrowed with an expression of rage that sent chills through me.

"Get over here," he demanded, his voice coarse with anger.

I wanted to tell him to go to hell. He didn't own me. But that wasn't true. Even without the non-disclosure agreement, Chase and I were bound to each other by this dangerous secret. We would be bound to each other by these lies for the rest of our lives—or, at least, until he was no longer President.

"I'll tear up that stupid NDA. I'll do whatever it takes to keep you here. But even if you decide to go back to L.A., I'm not giving up on you."

Chase spoke those words to me six weeks ago and I was just now beginning to understand the gravity of their meaning. I would never escape this secret as long as I was a threat to his career. Even if I wanted to, I would never escape Chase. And now that Teddy and Katherine knew about us, there was no way they would allow me to leave. They had to keep me close. This relationship was a bomb strapped to my chest and Heather Rodin at the *L.A. Times* was holding the trigger.

I let my dress fall to the floor as I approached Chase. He entered the hotel room from the balcony, his eyes locked on mine until we met in the center of the room.

"I knew what I was getting into," I said. "I just didn't expect for it to blow up in my face."

"It hasn't blown up yet. Gideon's been hounding the editor at the *Times* for weeks trying to figure out the angle on this piece. They're not talking, but that doesn't necessarily mean we have to panic," he said, as he draped his blazer around my shoulders. "But you're right. I did everything I could to erase our connection to *Black Tie Escorts* before you joined the campaign, but we have to prepare for the possibility that Heather dug something up. In fact, that's what tomorrow's meeting with Katherine and Teddy is about."

"It's a strategy meeting?" I replied, as he placed his hand on the small of my back and led me toward a red blanket laid across the carpet in the corner of the room. "What about Isa? Shouldn't he be there to give you the statistics on how all of this is going to affect you?"

Isa was the Campaign Statician—a position Chase made up just to get Isa on board. Isa graduated last year from Cornell with two masters degrees: one in political science and one in statistics. He had been receiving job offers from various politicians for over two years before his graduation. It was no surprise to many when he decided to work with Senator Chase Underwood. Chase was hard to resist.

"Lay down," he ordered, and I quickly knelt on the cashmere blanket and tossed his blazer aside. "Why do you think we're having the meeting? Isa gave me the numbers this morning. The numbers are based on historical data and none of the data is clear, but we're pretty certain I can still pull off a victory if…."

"If what?" I asked, as I lay down on my back and he stepped over me so he was straddling my legs as he looked down at me.

A candle had magically appeared in his hand and my fingers clutched the blanket as I watched him tip it over my belly.

"If you pretend to be with Teddy," he said, as the first drop of hot wax hit my skin right below my navel. I drew in a sharp breath as the wax stung my skin for just a moment before it cooled. "You can start pretending right now."

I could feel myself becoming engorged with pleasure as Chase let another drop of hot wax fall just below the first drop.

"But Teddy's so… wound up," I breathed.

"I think you'll find Teddy can be very charming. I have to make sure I leave you with an experience you'll be thinking about all day tomorrow," he replied, and a stream of wax hit the skin just above my pelvic bone and my body tensed as the liquid slid toward my lips. My hand immediately shot toward my crotch to keep the wax from burning me, but he warned me off. "Don't move."

I drew my hand back and was quite relieved when the wax rolled sideways onto my thigh. He stood above me, his shirt unbuttoned and a hungry look in his eyes.

"Close your eyes." I shut my eyes and he brushed against my arm as he sat next to me on the blanket. "Put your hands behind your head."

I clasped my hands behind my head and he immediately poured the wax over my nipple. I yelped with pain, which was quickly relieved as he brushed the warm wax away with his fingers and took my nipple into his mouth. He gently licked and sucked until the pain was gone.

"Better?"

"Yes, Sir."

He poured the wax over my other nipple and I gritted my teeth against the pain as I waited for him to relieve it again. He waited a bit longer this time before he wiped away the wax and soothed my pain with his mouth. He pulled away and I nearly reached out to pull him back, but I wasn't supposed to move.

"Turn over," he commanded. I flipped onto my belly and even the soft cashmere felt scratchy against my raw nipples. "Spread your legs and lift your ass."

I followed his orders, laying my face against the blanket as he positioned himself between my legs. He poured a fat stream of wax across my ass cheeks and I gasped.

"Oh, god!" I cried, as the wax dribbled down my ass and the backs of my thighs.

I could feel him moving behind me and suddenly his tongue was in my crease as his finger worked my clit. His tongue licked and massaged my opening and I tried not to squirm. The sensation of both areas being stimulated at once was unlike anything I'd ever felt.

"Oh, Chase," I whispered, trying not to raise my voice as I was still conscious of the open door leading to the balcony.

"Louder."

"Oh, Chase!" I cried into the blanket bunched up beneath my head. "Don't stop!"

"Louder!" he shouted, as my body quaked beneath him.

"Oh, Chase! *CHASE!*" I screamed, as he stimulated me beyond orgasm. "Please stop."

He didn't stop. He continued stroking my clit until I came again, even harder. When he finally drew away, I collapsed onto the blanket shaky and exhausted. He laid his body over mine, brushed my hair aside, and kissed the back of my neck as I attempted to catch my breath.

"What if someone heard me?" I whispered, as his fingers traced the curve of my hip.

He kissed me behind my ear before he replied. "It was worth it."

3

The knock on the door came just as I was slipping on my heels.

"Coming!" I shouted, and my heart raced as I approached the door of my hotel room.

I pushed the door open and found Teddy Holt standing before me in a crisp gray suit and no tie holding a copy of the *L.A. Times*. The headline read: UNDERWOOD'S TORRID AFFAIR WITH ESCORT.

"It's show time," he said, as he pushed his way past me into the hotel room.

He took a look around at the dozens of melted candles and wilted rose petals and didn't even flinch. Teddy was only a few months younger than Chase. From what Chase had told me, they had shared a dorm together at Yale and had been best friends since. Teddy had handled all of Chase's campaigns since he became Senator ten years ago at the age of thirty-two. It was no secret that Teddy intimidated everyone, but I'd been harboring a special kind of fear for him these past weeks. To see him standing before me as an ally brought forth a whole new set of emotions.

"Larissa," he said, as he held the paper out to me. "It's time to get this story straight, so it's time for you to start paying attention."

"I thought we were going to lunch to discuss this."

"I said pay attention, Larissa. We're getting our shit straight right now. There's a pack of reporters at every hotel entrance. We're not leaving here until you're ready. You got it, sweetheart? This all hangs on you. It's time to see if your acting skills are up to snuff. Can you handle that or am I wasting my fucking time?"

Fuck! I'm supposed to pretend I'm in love with this guy.

"Yeah, I can handle that," I replied, as I snatched the paper out of his hand.

"Good. Now, you don't have to read that shit because none of it's true. The truth is Chase ordered you from *Black Tie Escorts* as a birthday present for me and you and I fell in love. You got it?"

I wanted to punch him in his perfectly chiseled, condescending face.

"You can stop asking me that. I'm not a fucking child," I replied, and his mouth curled into an impressed half-smile.

"That's good to hear because I hate kids," he replied with a wink, and for a brief moment I could see what Katherine saw in him. "Are you taking mental notes? You'd better be taking mental notes, kid, because they're going to be asking you these kinds of questions."

And the moment passed. For the next two hours, Teddy grilled me on my past, present, and future. He wanted to know everything from my favorite color and food as a child to what I had for breakfast this morning and where I saw myself in five years.

"I don't know," I muttered, as I fidgeted with the corner of the newspaper in my lap.

Teddy sat across from me on the floor, but I refused to look at him. "What do you mean you don't know where you want to be in five years? It's a simple fucking question. And don't give me a bullshit answer."

"I can't tell you because it doesn't fit the story, okay?"

"Oh, I get it. You want to be shacking up with Chase, maybe with a bun in the oven and a new Mercedes SUV in the driveway."

I heaved a deep sigh. "Can we move on?"

"If we don't get this straight in the next hour, there will be no moving on, Larissa. Now answer the fucking question and make me believe the answer."

I think you'll find Teddy can be very charming. Was Chase being serious?

My hands began to shake as I imagined trying to convince anyone, much less a reporter, that I was in love with this bully. I tucked my hands beneath my legs to hide the trembling and Teddy reached for my left hand. I drew my hand behind my back and he tilted his head as if he was disappointed with my poor acting skills. After a brief staring contest, I relented and held out my hand.

He took it in his and looked up at me. "Go on."

I took a short pause to collect myself as I tried to remember all the sense memory and *"don't act, be"* bullshit I learned in acting class. I couldn't act like I was in love with Teddy. I had to *be* in love with him.

"I want to be with… with you," I began. "I don't care where we are or how many kids we have, or don't have, or how many fancy cars are in the driveway…. I just want to be with you."

I could see the slight rise and fall of Teddy's chest as he stared at me in silence. "Okay, I guess you're pretty good at that... stuff," he said, letting go of my hand and scooting back a few inches as if I had just admitted to having the swine flu.

He went on to tell me his life story; everything I needed to know about his childhood up to this morning when he had bagels and lox for breakfast—with Katherine.

"Shouldn't Chase and Katherine be here, I mean, you and Chase are supposed to be best friends. Isn't it natural to assume that Katherine and I have at least established a rapport, maybe even a friendship. Shouldn't we get those facts straight?"

Teddy raised his eyebrows as he looked at the carpet between us. "Yeah, that's not going to happen."

"Why? I thought it was show time. Isn't she part of the show?"

"Look, Larissa, you should know that Katherine is not very... fond of you. She sees you as a threat to Chase's career and she's pissed the fuck off at Chase for bringing you on as his PA. So, no, you are not going to meet with Katherine and there's no negotiating that."

For some reason, this piece of information disturbed me more than having to pretend to be in love with Teddy. I guess I had been under the illusion that Katherine and I would one day meet and she would thank me for taking care of her dear friend Chase. I never imagined she could hate me.

"Hey, if it makes you feel any better, it took her more than three years to warm up to Chase. And she still hates him most days."

"What's *wrong* with her?" I blurted before I could stop myself.

Teddy glared at me. "There's nothing *wrong* with her. In fact, you might want to take a page from her book and tone down the makeup, maybe try to at least *appear* a little less *escort-ish*."

"Excuse me? The campaign stylist told me to do my makeup like this. You're an asshole!"

"Well, that's the first time anyone's ever said that to me."

I shot up from the carpet and marched to the bathroom where my phone lay on the counter. I hit Chase's number and he picked up immediately.

"What's wrong?" he asked, and the sound of his voice immediately calmed me.

"I can't do this," I said, as Teddy entered the bathroom.

"Look, I'm sorry. That makeup thing was a low blow. I get it. Just hang up," Teddy pleaded.

A surge of bile stung my throat and I swallowed it down. "You're a horrible actor!" I shouted at him.

"Hey, what's going on over there?" Chase asked. "Are you okay?"

I glared at Teddy as his eyes beseeched me to hang up.

"Larissa, talk to me."

"I'm fine," I lied, as I looked Teddy in the eye. "I'm just really nervous. I think I'd feel better if I could get everything straight with Katherine."

Teddy's eyes widened and I couldn't help but smile. I had to let him know he no longer intimidated me. I was tired of being an actor in this play. I wanted to sit in the director's chair for once.

The pause on the other end of the line didn't bode well for my proposition. I tried not to tap my foot as I awaited Chase's response. Finally, he spoke.

"Come up to the penthouse."

4

My heartbeat throbbed in my skull as the elevator climbed toward the penthouse. I didn't think this through. I had no idea how I was going to approach Katherine. Should I attempt to be her friend when she clearly hated me? Should I keep it businesslike?

"Relax. She's not a fucking werewolf," Teddy said, as the elevator slowed to a stop.

"Uh, yeah, I think I would prefer a meeting with a werewolf right now," I replied, as the doors opened directly onto the penthouse antechamber.

The stark white wall in front of us boasted a surrealist painting I recognized from the art history course I took five years ago—just so I could share a class with my college boyfriend. I wished I could remember the artist. It would make a nice conversation piece to break the ice.

Maybe Katherine didn't like art. Maybe she hated it the way she hated me.

We turned the corner into the penthouse and found Chase sitting on a crisp white sofa with Katherine sitting next to him on the arm—above him. I was beginning to understand the dynamics of their relationship more by the second.

Chase stood as soon as he saw me, but I waited near the entrance for him to come to me. He planted a tender kiss on my cheek as I kept my eyes on Katherine's dark flowing hair and haughty expression.

"Larissa, you've met Katherine," Chase said, his voice a bit higher in pitch than usual.

"She's not here to meet me," Katherine said, casting a slow smirk in my direction. "She's here to assert her authority over this debacle."

"Katherine, please," Chase said, as he motioned for me to take a seat on the sofa. "Let's keep this civil."

I shook my head. "I'll stand, thanks," I said, before I turned to Katherine. "Kathy's right. You don't mind if I call you Kathy, do you?"

"Call me Kathy and I'll call you Larry."

"Okay… Well, *you're* right. I'm here to remind you all that I have the power to confirm or deny everything Heather wrote in that article and I'm tired of being a mouthpiece. For Christ's sake, I have the hardest job here: I have to pretend to be in love with *this*!"

Teddy did not appear amused by my jab at him, but Katherine let out a hearty guffaw.

"I guess you're not as dumb as Heather made you out to be," she said, as she stood from the sofa and took two steps toward me so we were face to face. "If you can dig deep down into your bag of *tricks* and put on the performance of your life, I think I might one day grow to tolerate you."

Bitch. Bitch. Bitch.

"Come now, ladies. There's no need for all this vitriol," Teddy chimed in. "We have to go down and face the hounds in twenty minutes. Let's get our stories straight and get the fuck down there."

Chase pulled me aside and put his lips to my ear. "Are you all right?"

"Peachy," I replied tersely, as I moved to get around him, but he grabbed my wrist to stop me.

"Larissa, whatever happens down there today, I want you to know that I'll be on the other side waiting for you—no matter how far apart we end up after the blast."

"What are you implying? Are we going to have to break up if that's what serves the campaign? Is that what you're saying?"

"I'm not saying that. I'm saying that, according to Isa's data, we may need to enact plan B if putting you and Teddy together doesn't work."

"What's plan B?"

Teddy sidled up next to me. "Plan B goes into effect if the press presents photographic evidence of you and Chase together. In that case, you'll have to go underground for a while."

"Underground?" I repeated his word, as if I could glean the meaning by saying it aloud. "What the fuck does that mean?"

When Chase and Teddy remained silent, Katherine answered for them. "It means you, my dear, will have to admit to seducing Senator Underwood during your long hours together and you will concoct a heartfelt, public apology to me right before you disappear."

"Disappear? What? Are you going to kill me?" I said, with a laugh and Chase took my hand and led me toward a corridor.

"Where are you taking me?" I asked, as I attempted to wrench my hand free from his grasp. "What? Are you going to throw me out the fucking window? Make it look like a suicide?"

"Stop it, Larissa!" he roared at me, as he led me into a bedroom and slammed the door shut. "Listen to me. Plan B means you'll get a new identity and we'll relocate you, somewhere off the grid, for at least six months until I'm in office and the scandal has died down."

"Six months?" I whispered, as I realized what was happening. "Plan B means throwing me under the bus and putting me in solitary confinement for six months? You agreed to this?"

He shook his head at me. "Larissa—"

"Stop saying my name!" I shouted. "I know Teddy's responsible for coming up with this, but I can't believe you're going along with it."

He took my face in his hands. "Larissa, please. It's the only way we're going to get through this in tact."

"It's the only way *you* three are going to get through this in tact!"

"Please," he whispered before his mouth was on mine.

I banged and shoved his chest, but he was too strong, and soon the gravity of his kissed pulled me under. He tore open my blouse and carried me to the bed. I undid his pants as he settled himself between my legs and yanked my skirt up. I gasped as he entered me.

"Fuck," he whispered, as he buried his face in my hair.

I moaned as he thrust in and out of me. "Oh."

"I fucking love you," he breathed into my ear. "I won't... I won't let them hurt you. I promise." His face hovered inches above mine as I gazed into his eyes. "Tell me you love me."

"I love you," I groaned, as his erection sunk deep inside me.

He kissed me slowly and deeply until I finally had to turn my face away to come up for air. His teeth sunk into my shoulder as his body shuddered and collapsed on top of me. His breath was hot and ragged against my skin as I wrapped my arms around his neck and held on as if he were my life raft. He buried his face in my neck, making no move to unearth his still throbbing cock from inside me. We lay like this for what seemed like no more than a minute before a knock on the door interrupted.

"Coming!" Chase shouted at the door, and we smiled at each other before he kissed me one last time.

5

An army of twelve Secret Service agents was lined up outside guarding the front doors of the hotel. The minute we stepped outside, the cameras flashed and I was blinded. Teddy wrapped his arm around my shoulder to guide me forward. He used his other hand to shield my face from the flashes of light. I wrapped my arm around his waist and leaned into him. I wasn't acting. I was terrified.

We approached a podium, which had magically appeared in front of the hotel. I wanted to bury my face in his shoulder, but Katherine and Teddy insisted I had to look strong but vulnerable. If I could pull this off, it would be the greatest performance of my life. All those years of drama and acting classes. All the faux tears I'd cried over faux tragedies. Surely, I could muster some faux strength in the midst of this very real tragedy.

"Good afternoon," Teddy said, and the microphone on the podium sounded perfectly crisp and blaringly loud as I gazed out across the shouting and ebbing sea of faces.

My eyes wandered further over the crowd until my heart stopped. The mob stretched all the way to the end of the block and beyond.

"Senator and Mrs. Underwood and Miss Jacobs will not be taking any questions today," Teddy's voice echoed in my ears as his hand fell from my shoulder.

Not answering any questions? Miss Jacobs? That's no way to address your supposed girlfriend, Teddy.

I turned around to confirm this new development with Chase, but he and Katherine were nowhere. They had been right behind Teddy and I as we approached the front door of the hotel. Now they were gone. They abandoned us. Chase abandoned me.

I looked to Teddy and the severe expression on his face as he glanced in my direction told me I was screwing this up. I didn't look strong. I didn't feel strong. I felt worthless.

Then I saw her. Heather Rodin stood in the front row of the pack of reporters holding up her hand to ask a question. And the anger returned. But I wasn't angry at Heather. She was just doing her job. I was angry at Teddy for making me think this was a press conference to clear Chase's name and make everyone believe Teddy and I were the ones having an affair. This wasn't a press conference. This was my public lynching. This was Teddy sewing a big, fat "A" on my chest in front of a crowd of thousands of people. This was me being exposed.

"Larissa: How much did Senator Underwood pay you for your first encounter together?" Heather's question whooshed past me as a roaring anger muffled my senses.

"I told you Miss Jacobs will not be answering any questions at this time," Teddy repeated his mantra over and over as my vision blurred with rage.

"You lied to me!" I shouted, and Teddy quickly motioned to the nearest Secret Service agent.

The same handsome agent I had ogled on my visit to Baltimore with Chase now had both my arms in a vice grip as he shoved me toward the hotel entrance. My feet glided over the concrete as he practically carried me toward the doors.

"Where's Chase?" I asked the agent, but he didn't answer. "Drew, please, where is he?"

I never addressed the agents by their names. He probably thought I didn't know his name because something changed in his face for just a brief moment. He shook his head as another agent grabbed my other arm and they both led me toward the elevator.

"How can you guys do this?" I whimpered, as the reality of how powerless I was at this moment finally hit me.

The tears rolled down my face in a never-ending stream of regret. I had trusted the wrong man. No, I had trusted the *most* wrong man. I had never screwed up this badly in my life and I had no safety net. I wouldn't be surprised if they had already cleaned my bank accounts to erase all ties to me. They were going to erase me. Anything so Chase could become the next president. Because the numbers showed that he still had a chance, but, obviously, only if I no longer existed.

"Larissa?" Drew's voice startled me as the elevator carried us upward. His young face was wrought with guilt.

"What?"

He opened his mouth to say something, but instead he shook his head. "Nothing."

"How could he do this to me?" I whispered to myself.

The elevator stopped at the penthouse and, for a moment, I allowed myself to think that Chase would be waiting on the other side of the doors. The elevator doors slid open and the antechamber was empty. They led me into the sitting area and there he was, sitting on the bottom step of the staircase.

"How—"

"Wait," he interrupted me, as he strolled across the black tile toward me. "Just be quiet for a moment."

He knelt in front of me and grabbed my left hand. "Larissa Jacobs, I love you more than I ever believed I could love someone."

My breath came in shallow gasps as the tears began to fall again.

"I know you must be very angry with me right now, but I'm asking you to trust that this is all going to work out. I'm asking you to trust me… for now and forever. Will you please marry me? Will you please let me love you for the rest of our lives?"

My stomach twisted inside me at the sight of him kneeling before me brandishing the ring I had picked out six weeks ago. Every piece of me wanted to scream *yes*, except for my shattered heart.

"You're sending me away," I said, gritting my teeth against this painful truth.

"I'll be back for you very soon."

"You said you wouldn't let them hurt me. What happened? What changed in the last twenty minutes?"

He glanced at my feet for a moment before he slipped his phone out of his pocket. He played a video of the two of us together in the hotel room last night, which appeared to have been taken from the hotel across the street.

"Teddy got this earlier, when we were making love," he said, the muscle in his jaw twitching as he stood.

"So this is plan B? Parade me in front of a horde of reporters then send me away to some remote cabin in Montana for six months. And I'm supposed to just wait for you?"

"Not six months."

"Then how long?"

"Three or four months tops. We need to at least wait until a few weeks after the inauguration… for things to die down."

Drew stepped forward. "Sir, the chopper's here."

I shook my head as I realized the chopper was there for me. "I can't believe this."

Chase squeezed my hand as he looked me in the eye. "Please let me put this ring on you."

"Do I even have a choice or is this some kind of mandatory witness protection program?"

"Of course, you have a choice," he replied with a glance at the ring.

I looked into his dark eyes, searching for a trace of deceit. Had I been wrong about him all along? Was this all a ploy to keep me loyal to him while I was in hiding?

No. He wasn't lying. We were both being tossed by this violent ocean of lies—lies we had both told. Lies we had told ourselves.

Drew cleared his throat. "Sir?"

"Just a minute," Chase replied, his eyes locked on mine as he awaited my answer.

I swallowed the fear lodged in my throat and nodded. "Yes. Yes, I'll wait for you."

He smiled like a boy with a new bicycle as he slipped the ring onto my finger. "You'll hear from me tonight." He kissed me, a deep, urgent kiss. "I love you," he said, as he rested his forehead against mine. "I'm going to make this up to you."

My chest ached as I tore myself away from him. "I know."

I turned away before I could change my mind and chased Drew up the staircase. A private elevator on the second floor of the penthouse delivered us onto the roof where a helicopter waited for us. I raced toward the helicopter, pushing aside worries about how I was going to get all my stuff to this secret destination. I climbed into the cabin and Drew helped strap me into the seat.

"Where are we going?" I shouted at him over the roaring squeal of the engine and the thwack of the rotors.

He shook his head before he strapped himself into the seat next to me. I didn't know if this meant he didn't know where we were going or he couldn't tell me, but I was starting to realize it didn't matter. Even if he knew, he wouldn't tell me.

The helicopter lifted off the roof and swept across the sky toward the west. I gazed at my ring and the way the light refracted off the stone and onto the ceiling of the chopper. Suddenly, I couldn't breathe. I tucked my hand under my thigh and turned my attention to the window. As I gazed at the Vegas strip below,

I thought of California and my ex-roommate Shane. He said I hit the jackpot when Chase picked me out of all the girls at the escort service. Suddenly, I was beginning to lose my taste for winning.

CHASE

PART IV: CLOSURE

1

When life hands you a precious gift, wrapped in a flashy bow, sometimes it turns out to be a boxful of lemons. That's how I felt about Chase's proposal, which came minutes after having our affair broadcast to millions of people yesterday. My father used to say, "When life kicks you down, grab it by the balls and twist as hard as you can." Right now, I didn't have the energy to make lemonade or grab anyone's balls. All I wanted at this moment was a comfortable bed and nine hours of sleep. The flight to Chase's villa in Tuscany had me jet lagged and I had an interview with Diane Sawyer in ten hours.

I followed Secret Service agents Drew Hardwick and Michael Pham up the marble staircase to the second floor of the lavish villa where I would be spending the next three to four months as Chase attempted to glue his campaign and possible presidency back together. I resisted the urge to run my fingers along the polished mahogany banister as I went over the interview script in my head. Gideon Vernon, Chase's public relations director, and Laura Greene, his speechwriter, had come up with a script for tomorrow's interview. It wasn't so much an interview as it was a chance for me to publicly deny my affair with Chase Underwood.

The whole thing reeked, but the campaign statician insisted it was the only option if they wanted any chance of salvaging

Chase's rapidly plummeting poll numbers. As my heels clicked against the wood floors in the corridor, I wondered if *I* was just a number. What if Chase had other mistresses in hiding?

That was way too much to fathom at this junction. I needed to rest up, do the interview, and try not to worry about what my parents would think when they saw me on ABC World News. This wasn't exactly the big break I'd been hoping for when I left home for Hollywood two years ago. I hated the thought of my mother turning to my father after seeing my interview and saying, "I told you so."

"This is your room, Miss Jacobs," Drew said, as he opened a set of tall double-doors revealing an enormous master suite that could easily fit my entire L.A. loft—four times.

"You can call me Larissa, Drew. I won't tell Diane Sawyer if you don't," I said, as I set my purse down on a chaise lounge and wandered across the sumptuous carpet. "This is huge. I don't think I need all this space. Are there any smaller rooms?"

Drew set my luggage down next to a massive armoire and glanced around. "This is nothing compared to his palace in San Diego. You'll be fine in here, but if you really need something smaller I can see if one of the servants will switch with you. Of course, Mike and I will have to bunk in the next room, wherever you decide to sleep."

"Servants? No, no, that's fine. I'll stay here. Thanks for bringing up my stuff."

"Yes, ma'am," he said with a nod of his head before he and Mike exited the room.

Ma'am? Miss Jacobs? I would have to talk to Drew about that later. Since he and Mike were the only agents assigned to guard me, and the only other people in this house who spoke English, we needed to at least be on a first name basis or the next three to four months would be very depressing.

I unzipped my suitcase and pulled out a nightgown to change into. I peeled off my lilac silk dress, which was now a wrinkled mess after so many unsuccessful attempts to fall asleep on the plane. As I tossed the dress aside, the bedroom door swung open.

Drew took one look at me in my bra and panties and scurried out of the room, slamming the door behind him. "I'm so sorry, Miss Jacobs!" he shouted through the door. "I was just bringing your new Italian cell phone. I'm so sorry!"

I quickly slipped on my nightgown and opened the door. "It's all right," I said, as Drew stared at his feet. "It's no big deal. I'm an actress, remember? I'm used to taking my clothes off in front of strangers in dressing rooms."

He smiled, but he still refused to look at me as he held out a shiny silver iPhone. "Here you go, ma'am."

I sighed as I took the phone from his hand. "Please call me Larissa. And please don't let things get awkward. I'm already freaking out about all this as it is."

He raised his head slowly and looked me in the eye. "Yes, m—I mean, Larissa. I guess I'll see you in the morning. Good night."

I laid the phone on the nightstand before I tucked myself in under the silky sheets and tried to shut off my mind, but images kept flashing behind my eyelids, clips of my relationship with

Chase: the satisfied smile on Chase's face as he made me come on our first "date" then dropped me off at my apartment without allowing me to return the favor; the first time I tasted him in my mouth; the day he brought a jeweler to my hotel room so I could pick out an engagement ring; then, of course, yesterday when he finally proposed. I wanted him here right now, inside me, putting his mouth on me.

I pulled up my nightgown and slipped my hand inside my panties. I writhed against the cool sheets as I imagined Chase's tongue exploring me.

"Ah…." I flipped onto my belly as I massaged my clit slowly then rapidly as I remembered my last encounter with Chase in my hotel room. "Oh, my god!" I screamed, and a knock at the door startled me. "Who is it?" I shouted, as I turned onto my back and pulled the covers up to my chin.

The thick doors muffled the soft plea in Drew's voice. I leaped out of bed and raced to the door, my crotch still throbbing with my fantasies of Chase.

I opened the door and Drew stood there, eyebrows raised in concern. "Is everything all right? I heard you scream."

"I'm fine," I whispered, as a maid walked past us toward the staircase.

"I'm sorry, but I was given strict orders to make sure you didn't attempt to… leave. And it sounded like you were struggling with something in there."

Yeah, struggling to stop thinking about Chase's hands on me.

"You thought I was trying to escape? From where, the balcony?"

Drew took in my incredulous impression and smiled. "I know it sounds stupid, but I can't take any chances."

"Fine. You're welcome to watch me from the chair if that will ease your paranoia. I'm going to sleep."

I strode back to the bed and climbed inside as Drew took a seat on the chaise. "I'll just sit over here," he muttered awkwardly. "You just feel free… to go right to sleep."

I pulled the fluffy down comforter up to my waist and leaned my head on my hand. "Do I make you nervous?"

He chuckled as he leaned forward and rested his elbows on his knees. "A little, yeah. Your fiancé practically threatened to kill me if I didn't take good care of you."

"Chase? He threatened you? What did he say?"

"He said if I didn't keep you safe or if I lost you it would be more than just my job on the line."

"Oh."

"Not a big deal. I'm used to high stakes jobs. Go to sleep. Once you're out, I'll call Michael in here to watch over you so I can get some sleep, too."

I turned over to face the window where the sun was just beginning to set. My first Italian sunset viewed from a cold bed with a Secret Service agent breathing down my neck. Not my idea of a romantic European getaway. I closed my eyes and tried not to obsess over the script running through my head. My eyeballs burned with exhaustion, but my mind refused to shut down. I nearly jumped for joy when my new Italian iPhone rang.

I snatched it off the nightstand and saw the call was coming in as "Unknown". I glanced at Drew and he nodded.

"Hello?" I answered.

"Larissa." Chase's voice was rich and soothing like a warm cup of cocoa. "Have you arrived at the villa?"

I couldn't hide my grin. "I just climbed into bed," I replied, and Drew took this as his cue to slip out of the bedroom and into the corridor. "I miss you."

"I can't tell you how much I wish I was there with you right now, watching the sunset with you, holding you in my arms, making love to you. What are you wearing?"

"Nothing," I said, as I turned on the speakerphone so I could tear off my nightgown.

"Good. Lay on your back and spread your legs."

I squirmed and kicked my panties off then spread my legs.

"Don't touch yourself yet," he continued. "Right now, I just want you to use your imagination."

"Okay," I said, my heart racing as I resisted the urge.

"I'm kissing your ear in that sensitive spot that makes you crazy."

"Mmm…."

"My hand is on your breast. I'm squeezing your nipple as I kiss your neck. Do you like that?"

"Yes."

"Your nipple is in my mouth and it tastes so sweet. You're making me so hard. I can't get enough of your taste."

I squirmed against the mattress. "I want you inside me. Please let me touch myself."

"Not yet. Arch your back for me so I can kiss your belly, baby, that spot just below your belly button." His voice sent shivers over my entire body. "You're skin is so warm and soft."

104

"Oh, Chase."

"My mouth is moving down... down... And now my mouth is on you, your clit is hard and pink and ready for me. Touch it."

My fingers glided through my wetness as I stroked myself.

"I'm licking and gently sucking. You're so wet. Mmm... You taste so fucking delicious."

"Turn onto your back," I said, pulling my hand away before I climaxed. "I want your cock in my mouth."

"Okay, but I want your tight little rosebud in my face so I can eat it up."

I turned onto my belly and pushed up onto my knees. "Your cock is so hard and so beautiful," I breathed. "I'm licking the tip. Oh, you taste amazing. So slippery and sweet."

"Oh, fuck," he groaned. "Take it all the way into your mouth, baby."

I moaned as my body began to spasm. "Pound it into my throat, Chase. Faster!" I massaged my clit vigorously as I bucked against the mattress. "Come in my mouth."

A deep groan vibrated the phone on the nightstand as my body quaked with an earth shattering orgasm. Chase's breath was amplified through the speaker and I suddenly realized that Drew probably heard our whole conversation.

"That was so fucking good," Chase said, as I touched the icon to take him off speakerphone.

"When are you coming?" I asked, as I pulled the comforter over me again.

"I believe I just came."

"You know what I mean," I replied. "I don't know how much longer I can stay here with no one to talk to."

"I'll be there in no more than five days. The election is the day after tomorrow, then, if I win, I'll need a couple of days for interviews and meetings before I can sneak out of here. I promise I'll be there as soon as I can."

I didn't know what to say. He hadn't mentioned it, but I suddenly felt as if the fate of our relationship hung on tomorrow's interview. If I did well, Chase could win the election and I might see him in five days. If I didn't do well, he could lose and I might get to see him sooner and, possibly, start planning our wedding.

"Larissa? What are you thinking?"

"Nothing. Just going over my lines for tomorrow."

"Honey, it's okay to be nervous. You're a great actress, but I don't want you to approach this like you would an acting job. I want people to see the real you. That's the Larissa they'll believe."

"You sound like my acting coach."

"Guess who I saw today?"

I paused for a moment as I tried to think of someone. "Your wife?"

"Very funny. I saw your mother."

"My mom? How did you see my mom?"

"Well, obviously, since the story broke yesterday there have been a thousand news vans parked outside your parents' home. They interviewed her briefly on Fox News."

"Great! Now she really hates me."

"She doesn't hate you, Larissa. She's your mother. You should call her to let her know you're okay."

"I thought I wasn't supposed to talk to her about us."

"You don't have to tell her the details of our relationship to let her know you're all right. Promise me you'll give her a call."

I could feel my face twisting into a sneer. "I'll try... after the interview. I'm too exhausted right now."

"Are you going to be okay tonight?"

"I'll be fine, but... can you stay on the line until I fall asleep?"

"Of course. Good night, princess."

The softness in his voice made my heart rise into my throat. I laid the phone next to my head on the pillow and closed my eyes. I tried not to think about my potential conversation with my mother and whether Drew was outside, listening to every sound I had made in the last twenty minutes.

"The very thought of you." Chase's voice came softly through the speaker as he sung me to sleep. I smiled as I listened, catching just a few lines before I drifted off.

2

Michael woke me at three in the morning to get ready for the interview, which would be recorded via Skype at five o'clock Italy time, or ten o'clock New York time. It would not be a live interview. This was the one stipulation Gideon refused to budge on when negotiating the terms. I didn't know if I liked this. A lot of editing could be done after the fact to make me look like more of a harlot than I already appeared to be.

Sometimes I wished I had never taken my roommate's offer to help me get a job at *Black Tie Escorts*. I might never have met Chase, but I also wouldn't have millions of people thinking of me as the filthy whore who seduced Chase Underwood, *Pretty Woman* style; and I certainly wouldn't be receiving death threats. No one cared, or probably even knew, that Chase was my first client at the escort service and that we didn't even have sex on our first "date".

Drew escorted me to the library where a laptop had been set up to record the interview. With so much on the line, you'd think they'd have sent a production crew out here to do my makeup and set up the lighting and professional cameras to make everything look perfect. Maybe they *wanted* me to look cheap?

I sat in an armchair next to an ornately carved desk as Michael pointed the laptop's webcam at me. My skin looked a bit yellow in the glow of the lamplights, but I supposed it was better than looking washed out by the daylight. I glanced at Michael as he scooted between the desk and me so he could connect me to the production assistant in New York. Once the connection was made, he stepped aside and I found a bewildered guy with a pointed chin and absurdly long nostrils staring back at me through the screen.

"Miss Jacobs, can you hear and see me?" he said in a feminine voice.

"Yes, can you hear and see *me*?"

"I gotcha. I'm Daniel, by the way," he said, as his eyes turned downward to look at something on the anchor desk, possibly Diane Sawyer's notes. He looked up again, seeming even more bewildered. "Oh, shit. I don't have Simon's notes."

"Who's Simon?" I asked, as my stomach gurgled with hunger and anxiety. I hadn't eaten since before yesterday's flight.

"Simon is our field producer. Shit! Where are those notes?"

"Is this going to affect the interview?"

"Yes! Yes, yes, yes! This is definitely going to affect the interview. Shit, shit, shit! I am *so* fired."

"Calm down, Daniel," I said, as he scoured the surface of the anchor desk. "What kind of notes are you looking for?"

Please don't find the notes. Please call off the interview.

"Oh! Here they are!" he shrieked, and the tiny laptop speakers crackled as he held up a thin manila envelope. "That was close."

"Yeah... that was close," I muttered, trying not to look too disappointed.

"Okay, so I already went over the specifics with Gideon, but I'll go over them with you now."

He rambled on for more than twenty minutes about Diane's interview style and how I should try not to fidget and a billion other tidbits on how to make the interview more compelling and visually appealing. Some of this stuff I had already learned in the many camera classes I'd taken. Some of it was just ridiculous, like making me change my ivory silk blouse because it looked too similar to Diane's.

"Are you ready?" Daniel asked, and I nodded, too annoyed with him to even respond. "Great. We start rolling in twelve minutes. Sit tight."

I sat back in the chair then immediately sat up again as I remembered Daniel's advice on slouching. Then I sat back again as I realized I didn't have to worry about any of that stuff for another twelve minutes. My leg bounced uncontrollably, a subconscious attempt to rid myself of all this nervous energy.

Drew entered the library and noticed the panicked expression on my face. "Just checking to make sure Mike set everything up," Drew said. I nodded and he chuckled. "You'll do fine. I'll be right outside if you need me."

He was just being polite, just trying to ease the alarming anxiety building inside me, but I was slightly annoyed by his interruption. I turned back to the laptop as he closed the door. I had to focus on the script. Not that I would forget my lines, but there was no guarantee Diane would ask any of the questions I was prepared to answer.

"Standby, Larissa." Daniel's voice blasted through the speakers, but all I could see was the empty anchor desk.

Diane appeared from the left side of the screen and settled into her seat at the desk. My heart pounded as I watched her and

Daniel leafing through the notes while a hair stylist smoothed every shiny strand of hair on her head. My leg began bouncing again and I quickly sat up and centered my face in front of the camera.

Daniel and the hair girl stepped away and Diane cleared her throat before she looked into the camera, straight at me. "Can someone please bring me some water?" she asked, as she sat up straight then leaned forward slightly.

"Roll tape," said an off-camera voice.

A hushed pause followed then came Diane's soothing voice.

"We spoke with Larissa Jacobs today to give her a chance to clear the air surrounding the shocking accusations of her affair with presidential candidate and California Senator Chase Underwood. Larissa's version of the scandal that has torn the presidential debate wide open just two days before Election Day may come as a surprise to those who read the version printed in the *Los Angeles Times* yesterday. Today, Larissa has agreed to a candid interview with no restrictions in hopes that the nation can move swiftly past these allegations before the coming election."

"Cut."

The version printed in the Los Angeles Times? You mean, the truth? I tried not to shake my head in dismay at the lies I was about to tell on national television.

It took nearly thirty minutes to setup the new camera angle, which displayed both Diane and the TV screen to her left where my frightened face suddenly appeared. I took a deep breath as I tried to adjust my expression and my posture to appear more confident.

"Roll tape."

Diane took a moment to collect herself before she looked directly at my face on the screen. "Larissa, you have been accused of destroying Senator Chase Underwood's chances at what had been dubbed a near certain presidential victory and possibly his entire career. The senator's supporters have called you a whore. Conspiracy theories have cropped up about your being a saboteur working for the Republican party in an attempt to discredit the senator. Supporters of Underwood's opponent, Vice President Heller, have called you a godsend. Do *you* think you have destroyed Senator Underwood's presidential career?"

I took a beat, as Daniel instructed me to, before I answered. "No, Diane, I don't believe I've destroyed the prospects of Senator Underwood's presidential bid. I believe that the facts, and I, have not been accurately portrayed and, once the country knows what truly happened, Senator Underwood will be elected president on Tuesday."

"Would you care to tell us what *truly* happened?"

This is it. Make it good, Larissa.

"Well, this all began with a somewhat foolish and desperate decision I made in August, while I was still living in Los Angeles. It was the end of the month and the rent was coming due on the apartment I shared with my roommate." I paused so I wouldn't sound like I was rambling nervously. "I had just been let go from my job as a children's party entertainer and my roommate offered to get me a position with the escort service where he had been employed for three years."

"And you accepted your roommate's offer?"

"Foolishly, yes. My first day on the job was August 29th and that was the day I met Senator Underwood."

"Are you saying Senator Underwood was your first client?"

If I were telling the truth, yes, that's what I would say.

"No, Teddy Holt was my first and only client. Senator Underwood merely booked me to accompany Teddy to a black tie gala."

Diane pretended to look confused by my response. "Are you saying Senator Underwood *purchased* you as a date for his campaign manager Theodore Holt?"

"Well, yes, initially the gala was going to be the end of it, but Teddy and I never actually went to the gala. We skipped out on the event and had the most amazing night on the cliffs of Malibu, where we fell in love."

"That sounds like quite the fairy tale ending. However, I'm sure everyone would like to know... at any time, did you accept payment for sexual favors from either Senator Underwood or Teddy Holt?"

"I quit the escort service after my first day on the job and I never received a paycheck, so the answer to that question is no."

"Did you, at any time, engage in a sexual relationship with Senator Chase Underwood?"

"I have never had a sexual relationship with Senator Underwood."

"There are people who consider the escort business a cover for prostitution. Larissa, be honest with me, don't you find the idea of being purchased as a date, even if you weren't paid and no sexual favors were exchanged, the *tiniest* bit degrading."

It took every bit of resolve not to tell her to go to hell and that she was the only one who made me feel degraded, but I kept my cool.

"That's a good question, Diane, and I can understand how some would perceive the escort industry as a prostitution ring dressed up in an expensive suit. However, I'm afraid I don't know much about the industry since I never actually finished a full day of work. My first day on the job was spent being interviewed by Senator Underwood and arranging for me to meet Teddy before the Baltimore visit."

"Does the circumstances of your meeting with Teddy bother you at all?"

"Of course, it does," I replied. "I still deal with the shame that my financial distress caused me to make such a desperate employment decision. But people meet and fall in love under much stranger circumstances every day. At some point, you have to stop judging yourself for something that resulted in such fortuitous consequences."

Diane took a rather lengthy pause as she examined her notes. "Larissa, Heather Rodin at the L.A. Times has said she would like to sit down and speak with you one on one. She has even expressed a desire to apologize for any harm she may have caused. She said, and I quote, 'Larissa is a smart girl who obviously is not afraid to *chase* after what she wants. I think we have a lot in common and might be great friends under different circumstances.' Do you feel the same way about Heather? Do you think you two could ever put all this behind you and be friends?"

I couldn't help but smile as I attempted to temper the anger blistering inside me. "I would gladly accept an apology from

Heather, but, no, I don't think Heather and I could ever be friends. Heather may have some redeeming qualities as a person, and I'm sure she has worked very hard to achieve her position at the *Times*, but the misinformation she printed yesterday gives me the impression that she is either very untrustworthy or unstable."

"That's a damning accusation to make about an, albeit upcoming, respected journalist."

"Diane, let me tell you something about Heather Rodin," I began, as I geared up to let loose the zinger Gideon had dug up on Heather to discredit her. I took a deep breath. "Heather Rodin fabricates sources. Her exposés are just a notch above tabloid trash. Last year, Heather Rodin wrote eight exposés, one of those was on Congresswoman Carol Jennings from Colorado and the misappropriation of federal wildlife preservation funds. She did another exposé on Nebraska State Senator Phillip Hardy's alleged inappropriate relationship with a female coworker. On both occasions, she fabricated information, citing anonymous sources that did not exist."

Diane furrowed her brow. "Cut," she muttered, before she turned to someone off-camera. "Why isn't any of this in my notes?" I waited for the interview to resume for more than thirty minutes before Diane returned looking a bit wild-eyed. "We will have to confirm your accusations before any of that can be aired," she said, in a very friendly and reassuring tone. "For now, we'll continue the interview."

"I understand," I replied.

Diane settled into her interviewer pose and the cameras rolled. "Larissa, we also spoke with Katherine Underwood who confirms your story. Her official statement to ABC News states that your romantic relationship with Teddy Holt was kept under wraps so as not to detract any momentum from the campaign, should the circumstances of your meeting become public. Katherine has stated that the two of you have become great friends and categorically denies that your relationship with her husband is anything but appropriate. Do you have anything you'd like to say publicly to Katherine Underwood?"

"Katherine and I only spoke briefly before I was whisked away into hiding after receiving multiple death threats. She knows how sorry I am that my relationship with Teddy has caused a whirlwind of misinformation and bad press, but I would like to take this opportunity to apologize once again. I am confident that Americans will accept the truth in time to make the right choice for our country. Senator Underwood has worked very hard over the past decade to make California and this nation a better place for all of us. I'm sure Americans will see past the rhetoric and speculation to focus on the hard truth when they cast their ballots on Tuesday."

Diane asked a few more questions about my upbringing and my acting career before she thanked me for the interview and, right on cue, Drew entered the library to escort me down to the dining room for breakfast.

My stomach roared with hunger as soon as I smelled the scrambled eggs with crispy prosciutto, the fragrant melon–basil salad, and steamy cups of espresso. Drew pulled out a chair for me to take a seat at the long dining table.

"You're not going to eat?" I asked, as he made his way toward the kitchen door.

He squinted his blue eyes as if he was considering my question. "I just don't want to be alone right now," I added.

He turned around and took a seat in the chair across from me. "I was going to relieve Mike from the rear property entrance, but he can wait."

"Thanks," I said, as I popped some scrambled eggs into my mouth. "Oh. My. God. These are delicious. I'll bet Chase has Mario Batali working in the kitchen."

"I made the breakfast," Drew replied, with a shy smile. "His last chef quit and he hasn't bothered hiring a new one; too busy with the campaign. I figured the least I could do, after that Oscar-worthy performance, was make you something to eat."

I squirmed in my seat as I began to imagine him in the kitchen, cooking for me, naked. I crammed more eggs into my mouth and hastily washed them down with the rest of my fresh-squeezed orange juice and espresso.

"Thirsty?" he remarked.

"You have no idea."

3

I spent nearly two days shut inside my room, trying to resist my desire to talk to Drew. He continued to bring exquisite meals to my room even though I had insisted I didn't need him to cook for me. I wanted to hear Chase's voice. Every time I touched myself I thought of Chase, but this morning Drew's face had flashed in my mind. I decided then that I would hold off until I saw Chase in three or four days—*if* I saw Chase in three or four days.

I sat cross-legged on the floor of the bedroom, just inside the doors leading to the balcony and watched the sunset. The polls had been open for a few hours on the other side of the Atlantic Ocean. I should be watching the news coverage on my phone, but I couldn't stand seeing all the interspersed clips of my interview with Diane Sawyer and Heather Rodin's venomous reaction. I had destroyed Heather Rodin's career. Actually, she had done that on her own when she fabricated her sources, but it didn't make me feel any less awful.

A knock came at the door and Drew entered. "I brought you the laptop in case you want to watch the coverage on something bigger than a four-inch screen."

"Thanks. You can set it down on the bed."

He laid the computer on the bed and stared at me for a moment. "I was senior class president in high school."

I smiled. "Is that supposed to impress me?"

"Of course," he replied, as he joined me on the carpet. "I was embroiled in a big scandal just before that election. I'd been caught ditching home economics two days in a row."

"Quite the scandal. How did you ever manage to recover from that one?"

"I paid off my Home Ec teacher to dispute the findings."

I looked at him questioningly and he grinned.

"Okay, the truth is I won because I was extremely good looking. No one cared if I ditched class. There weren't enough goody-goodies in the school to outweigh those who wanted to bask in the glow of my popularity."

I chuckled weakly. "I get what you're trying to say, Drew, but this is a whole other level of deception going on here. I just wish I could be honest. I wish everyone knew that Chase and Katherine's relationship is a sham. I wish they knew that Chase and I are in love. That's what I wish the most. I hate the secrecy more than the scandal."

"Are you afraid he's going to leave you if he loses?"

"What do you mean? Do you know something I don't know?"

"No, no, I was just asking," he replied, shaking his head emphatically. "It's just… I'd hate to see you get hurt after all of this."

"Well, I would really hate to get hurt after all of this. This is definitely the most complicated relationship I've ever been in."

"To be fair, what did you expect? He's Chase 'Fucking' Underwood."

I shrugged. "I guess I didn't expect to be hidden away in some remote corner of Europe, staring out a window at the most beautiful sunset I've ever seen, alone."

"Hey," he said, as he nudged my shoulder. "You're not alone."

I turned to him and his smile made my stomach flip. The hair on my arms prickled as I thought of what I had been doing in the shower this morning when Drew's face flashed in my mind. Suddenly, his face was just inches away. His boyish features and round blue eyes were getting closer; so close I could feel the warmth of his breath.

I placed my hand on his chest and pushed him back. "I'm sorry, Drew. I can't do that."

He placed his hands on the floor behind him and leaned back. "I'm sorry. It's just that I find you very attractive and I think you deserve to be with someone who can give you everything you want; someone who can give every part of themselves to you."

I stood from the floor and went to the bed where I scooped up the laptop. "Let's watch some exit poll coverage."

Ten hours later, at five o'clock in the morning Italy time, the call was made and Chase was declared the next President of the United States of America. The deciding factor was the narrow victory he eked out in North Carolina, a state that he had called home for nearly five years after college. It seemed his former neighbors felt more betrayed by his alleged affair than anyone else, though not enough to overrule his popularity.

I closed the laptop and stood from the floor.

"Don't you want to see the victory speech?" Drew asked, as he stood.

"Not really." I didn't want to listen in vain for a *thank you* that would never come. As I approached the bed, my phone rang.

"Larissa," Chase whispered. "I'll see you in two weeks."

Before I could open my mouth to respond, the line went dead.

I placed the phone on my nightstand as Drew made his way to the door. "Are you hungry or are you going to hit the sack?" he asked.

I stared at the phone for a moment. *Two weeks?* What had changed since we spoke two days ago? I opened the nightstand, tossed the phone into the drawer, and slammed it shut. "I'm starving."

I didn't hear from Chase at all for three days, which I opted to spend walking through the vineyard behind the villa rather than cooped up in the bedroom. My phone rang as I passed the infinity pool next to the tennis courts.

"You've been busy," I said, as I answered.

"Of course, I've been busy. Honey, are you okay? Are you upset with me?"

He sounded exhausted, and for that simple fact I decided not to chew him out for leaving me waiting for three days without a single word.

"I'm fine, just lonely. I thought you were supposed to be here today or tomorrow. What happened?"

"I know I was supposed to be there, but Teddy couldn't clear a large enough chunk of time for me to fly out there."

I sat on a cushioned deck chair and, for a brief moment, considered jumping into the sparkling pool, phone and all. Maybe the chlorinated water could wash away all this uncertainty.

"I miss you," I whispered, as I wiped away the first tears. "I don't have anyone to talk to here except for Drew and I think he wants to do more than talk so every time I see him I feel awk—"

"What did you say?"

I paused a moment. "I said I don't have anyone to talk to here."

"Did you say Drew has been hitting on you?"

The anger in his voice made my heart stutter, but something about it also got me hot.

"No, I didn't say that. He didn't hit on me."

"Then why did you say you think he wants to do more than talk?"

"It's not like that. I just get the feeling he's got a bit of a crush on me. He hasn't acted on it, I swear."

"He has a *crush* on you? Larissa, this is a grown man. Men don't have crushes; they have urges. I'm coming over there."

"No! You don't have to do that. Everything's fine. Do what you need to do. I swear. Everything is *just* fine."

Chase let out a chuckle. "Larissa, I'm not going to kill the man. I'm just going to have a chat with him, man to man. That's all. I'll see you in twelve hours."

4

This was not the kind of visit from Chase I had been fantasizing about. If he scared Drew off, I might not have anyone to talk to for the next three to four months. Or, worse, what if he fired him?

I showered and shaved every inch of my body then I spread the pineapple-flavored lotion Chase loved so much all over me. I paid extra attention to my crotch and before I knew it I was nearing orgasm. I yanked my hand back before I could climax. It had been four days since the incident in the shower where Drew's face flashed in my mind. I wanted to save this pent up energy pulsating throughout my entire body for Chase.

A knock came at the bedroom door just as I was attempting to zip up my little black dress. "The president just arrived," Mike shouted through the door.

The president? Just the phrase got me hot and bothered.

I raced to the door and opened it wide. "Mike, can you zip me up?"

Mike's eyebrows scrunched together as he backed away from me.

Drew smiled. "I'll do it."

"No!" I shrieked. "No, that's all right. I'll do it myself. I was just… kidding. I don't need help. See?"

Drew eyed me suspiciously as I struggled to zip myself up. With a shake of his head, he and Mike set off to greet Chase. I followed behind them, attempting to yank my zipper up as I walked. I finally got it up when we were halfway down the staircase, just as Chase entered through the enormous double doors.

There was something different about him since the last time we were together five days ago. It wasn't a physical change in appearance. It was something else. Maybe it was just my perception of him, but he appeared more... commanding. *Way* more sexy, if that were possible. I wanted to jump on top of him and make love to him right on the marble floor, but he wasn't even looking at me. He only had eyes for Drew.

"Chase," I called to him as I descended the last few steps, but he continued to glare at Drew. "Honey, look at me."

Chase turned to me and his eyes softened. I threw my arms around his neck and kissed him hard. He wrapped his arms around me and pulled my body against his as he returned my kiss with more passion than I had ever felt from him before. I wanted to rip his clothes off right here, but he soon pulled away.

"What's this?" he asked, as he looked over my shoulder at my back. "Your dress is unzipped."

"Is it? Oh, geez, I guess I was having trouble reaching it."

"I offered to zip it up for her, but she refused my help."

Chase glared at Drew and I latched onto his arm then twirled around so my back was to him. "I wanted you to do it," I said. "Please zip me up."

My skin prickled as his fingers grazed my bare back. He pulled the zipper up and laid a soft kiss on my neck, as if he were trying to send Drew a message that I was his. Something about that idea made me nervous and I turned around to face him.

"Come upstairs with me," I whispered, putting on my best come-hither expression.

He kissed my forehead before he stepped away. "You go ahead and I'll be up in a few minutes."

I panicked as he strode toward Drew and beckoned him into the dining room. If he fired Drew it would be my fault. I had to go after him.

"Wait!" I called out, as I chased after them.

I entered the dining room and Chase glared at me as if I was intruding. Drew stared at the floor like a child waiting to be chastised.

"Larissa, can I please have a moment alone with Drew? I'll be up in just a moment."

"No, I can't wait. I need you upstairs *now.*"

I didn't blink as Chase narrowed his eyes at me. "Fine," he finally relented before he turned to Drew. "We'll talk later."

I held out my hand to him and he brought it to his lips. "I can't resist the princess who convinced the nation to elect me, can I?"

"You're not getting off that easily," I replied. "You and I have some things to discuss."

He smiled as he followed me out of the dining room then up to the bedroom. He closed the door behind him and we stared at each other in silence. I didn't know what he was thinking, but I was thinking about the next three to four months.

"Why do I have to stay here if you've already won the election? I feel like a fucking pris—"

"You don't."

"I don't—? What?"

"You don't have to stay here anymore, at least, not for three or four months as we had originally planned."

My mouth dropped wide open. "What? Are you going to tell me now I only have to stay for two months? Ugh! You make me so mad sometimes! Why are you laughing? This isn't funny!" He grabbed my hand as he attempted to stifle his laughter, but I yanked my hand back. "I can't do this anymore, Chase. I don't want to be here. Do you understand me? You can't keep me here. I swear to you I will find a way to escape."

He finally composed himself, though he was still smiling. "Larissa, I'm not leaving you here for two months. I'm not even leaving you here for two days. I have a plane coming to pick you up tomorrow morning to fly you back to L.A."

Suddenly, the walls began to pulsate as I realized he was finally through with me. He was sending me back where I came from and he was going off to Washington D.C. to find someone better; someone who wasn't tainted by this scandal.

"So that's it? You got what you wanted; now I'm getting tossed aside like yesterday's news? Is that what's going on here?"

"What? No, that's not what's going on here."

He stepped toward me and I stepped backward until the back of my legs bumped into the side of the bed, but he kept coming at me.

"Then what's going on here? Huh? Why did you fly all the way out here to tell Drew to back off if you were just planning to dump me in L.A.?"

He stopped in front of me so our noses were inches apart. "I'm here to tell you that I'm quitting."

"You... quitting? Quitting what?"

"I have a meeting with the Speaker of the House tomorrow to discuss my resignation as president-elect. I'm quitting politics... for you."

"You can't do that. You've worked too hard for this. What are you *thinking*?"

He placed his strong hands on either side of my waist and pulled my body against his. "I'm thinking a spring wedding in L.A."

"What? You're talking crazy. Have you even slept?"

"When you told me Drew had a crush on you I realized that this façade I'm asking you to put on has put me in danger of losing you, and that's when I realized I'd rather lose the presidency than live the rest of my life without you. It's just as simple as that."

"Oh, my god. You're serious."

"As a fucking heart attack. I've never met anyone as fiercely loyal and trusting and beautiful as you, Larissa. I want the world to know not just that I love you but that you love me, because that's what makes me the luckiest bastard in the world."

"After what happened on Tuesday, I think everyone already knows that."

He smiled as he scooped me up in his arms and laid me on the bed. He gazed at me for a moment, taking in the curve of my breasts and hips, before he lay next to me. He traced his finger over the bridge of my nose, over my lips, into the hollow of my neck, and between my breasts. I sighed as his fingers lightly caressed my belly. I had been craving his touch and here he was, giving me everything I craved and more.

His lips fell on mine tasting like the sweetest candy. His tongue explored my mouth the way it had explored my body so many times before. I felt as if I was falling into the bed, sinking deeper and deeper into this dream that wasn't a dream.

I reached down to undo his belt and he pushed my hand away.

"That will have to wait," he said, as he sat up. "I have a plane to catch if I want to make that meeting tomorrow."

"That's it?" I muttered, unable to hide the disappointment of my unfulfilled need. I wanted him inside me. I wanted to feel the weight of him on top of me.

He chuckled as he rose from the bed. "That is definitely not *it*. I have big plans for you when we get back to L.A. I already had your old roommate deliver your things to my house in Pacific Palisades. We're going to have plenty of time to execute those plans once I join you there tomorrow evening." He planted a soft kiss on my lips then made for the door. "I take it I can leave Drew to his schoolboy fantasies. I don't have anything to worry about there, do I?"

"Of course not, but what about all the people who threatened to lynch me back home?"

"I already hired a private security team. You have nothing to fear. I'll see you tomorrow. Oh—wear that pink dress you wore to the AMA benefit."

As he left the room, I collapsed onto the bed and stared at the vaulted ceiling above me. My crotch throbbed with unfulfilled desire. I slid the hem of my dress up a few inches then stopped. I could wait until tomorrow night.

5

The plane landed in Los Angeles at five p.m. local time. As soon as I debarked, a helicopter was already on standby outside Chase's private hangar. Drew carried my luggage across the tarmac and heaved it into the helicopter where two enormous fellows in crisp black suits, my private guards, awaited me.

"I guess you won't be needing my services anymore," he shouted over the thumping of the rotors.

"Thanks for not treating me like a prisoner," I shouted back before we hugged.

He held on longer than I would have allowed him to otherwise, but I had to cut the guy some slack after the wrath I almost unleashed on him yesterday. He finally let go and I climbed inside the helicopter. As the chopper lifted off then banked toward the ocean, I breathed a deep sigh of relief to finally be home. The skyscrapers and the smog were my security blanket and these months on the road had taken their toll on me. I was exhausted. All I wanted was to get home, to my new home with Chase, and fall asleep in his arms.

The helicopter approached the hills of Pacific Palisades and one of the burly bodyguards turned to me. "Miss Jacobs, can you please put this on? Boss's orders."

He handed me a black satin blindfold. "What is this for?" I asked, as I took it from his hand.

"I'm sorry. Mr. Underwood didn't share that information with me. Please put it on."

I slipped the blindfold over my head and an anxious feeling settled into the pit of my belly as I felt the helicopter descend. The chopper soon landed and I unbuckled my seatbelt.

"I'm going to take your arm to help you get out," the guard said, as he grasped the crook of my arm and guided me out of the helicopter onto what felt like cool sand.

He led me forward and I listened for sounds of humans, but all I heard was the sound of waves crashing on my left. I trudged through the sand, trying to ignore the grittiness of the sand in my heels. We walked a few more yards before he stopped.

"Are we here?" I asked, but no one answered. "Can I take this off now?"

I heard the distinct sound of sand crunching as someone approached on my right side. I turned my head instinctively, but couldn't see anything. I flinched slightly as someone's hands touched my head and slipped off my blindfold.

Chase stood before me in a black tux with no tie and a crazy grin on his face. On my left, rows and rows of white chairs were filled with sharply dressed people with their backs toward me. Candles and rose petals lined the aisle between the rows of chairs. Then someone waved at me from the altar. Even backlit by the gorgeous sunset, I still recognized the ravishing gentleman in the tux: Shane, my ex-roommate, was standing on the bride's side. Teddy stood on the groom's side wearing a knowing smile.

"What is this?"

Chase took my hands in his and looked me in the eye. "This, my love, is for you. I know we can't legally get married until the divorce is final, and I promise to give you a huge wedding when that happens, but I wanted to show you that I'm serious by declaring my love to you in front of all the people who matter the most to us. So... do you still want to marry me, even after everything I've put you through?"

I looked back and forth between the altar and Chase's anxious face. "I'm not dressed to get married," I whispered, referring to my sand-filled heels and the pink A-line tank dress he asked me to wear today.

"What are you talking about? You look radiant as ever. Do I have to get on my knees again?"

He started to kneel and I grabbed his arm to stop him. "No! You'll ruin your tux."

"Is that a yes?"

I bit my lip as I nodded.

"Woo-hoo!" he shouted, as he lifted me and spun me around.

I didn't know it was possible to feel this deliriously happy. All I had known for the past two years was hundreds of rejections and low-paying jobs that eventually led to the mountain of debt and my job at the escort service. I thought back to the night before my first day as an escort. I had lain in bed and contemplated the wreck my life had become and how my parents were right all along. I wished they were here now to see this.

Chase put me down and grinned as he gazed into my eyes.

"What are you grinning at?"

"You'll see," he said. "Stay right here."

He set off down the aisle, I presumed to take his place on the altar. When he reached the front row of seats, he bent over to speak to someone. An older gentleman in a gray suit stood up and turned around. My father's face beamed as he caught sight of me.

I bit my lip so hard I drew blood as I tried to hold back the tears, but it was no use. He made his way toward me and I saw that he also was having trouble holding himself together. I raced to him and threw my arms around him.

"Dad!"

"Sweetheart. You look so beautiful," he said, his voice thick with the pain of two years absence. "I'm so proud of you. You really let Diane Sawyer have it."

I chuckled as I wiped away my tears. "Is Mom here?"

My father nodded as he held out his arm for me. "She's right up front. Are you ready?"

I grasped his arm as a harpist began to play "The Very Thought of You." I kicked off my heels and my feet sank into the cool sand. We began our walk down the aisle and I couldn't believe how many familiar faces I found in the seats: Shane's boyfriend Jackson Kim; my old boss at the escort service, Jessica Broom (whose business was rumored to have doubled since the scandal broke); Chase's campaign statician, Isa, and his new wife, Nina; politicians I had met during the campaign. Drew winked at me from his seat. We reached the front row and I was surprised to see Katherine Underwood sitting next to my mother and wearing what appeared to be a genuine smile.

The look on my mother's face, a mixture of sadness and pride, made my heart ache as she blew me a kiss. We reached the altar and my father kissed my cheek before he took his seat. Shane winked at me and I knew in his head he was screaming, *"Jackpot!"*

Chase held out his arm and an uncontrollable grin stretched across my face as I latched onto him. He kissed my forehead then leaned over and whispered in my ear, "So worth it."

Our bedroom in the house on the edge of the cliff had the most gorgeous view of the moon over the ocean.

"I can't believe you live here," I said, as I walked through the master suite.

I ran my fingers over the smooth wood of the four-poster bed as I made my way toward the terrace. Chase followed me outside and wrapped his arms around my waist.

"I can't believe *you* live here," he said, as he nuzzled my neck and kissed my ear.

I turned around and all the desire I had been suppressing these past few days poured out of me as I kissed him. He kissed me back hungrily and I realized he had been waiting for this moment, too. Without warning, he scooped me into his arms and carried me toward a wooden staircase leading down from the terrace to the beach. I kissed his neck and tasted the salt-spray that had battered us during the ceremony. We reached the bottom of the staircase where he placed me down in the sand and quickly unzipped the back of my dress as I unbuckled his belt.

The moonlight painted silver streaks across his strong shoulders as we stood before each other completely nude. He pulled me close and his erection pressed against my belly as his lips fell softly over mine. The smell of the ocean and Chase's scent mixed together were a heady combination and I wanted him inside me now.

"Take me," I pleaded. "Right here. Please."

"To the water," he said, as he took off running toward the waves.

I chased after him, laughing as I tried to catch up. He beat me to the water and we both gasped as the cold waves penetrated down to our bones.

"It's too cold!" I shouted, as I turned to leave, but he grabbed my hand.

"I'll keep you warm."

He pulled me further in and my eyes widened with shock as each icy wave crashed into me. We slogged through the squishy sand until we were waist deep. He lifted me and I wrapped my legs around his waist. He slid into me and I moaned, suddenly forgetting all about the temperature of the water.

"Oh, Chase. I've been waiting for this."

He leaned me over so my back lay across the surface of the water as he slipped slowly in and out of me. "Ah," he groaned, as his hand glided over my belly and he cupped my breast in his hand.

He rolled my nipple between his fingers and I screamed with pleasure. His cock filled me so perfectly and completely. The ocean ebbed beneath me, delivering me toward ecstasy as he sank in and out, drowning in me

"I don't want to come yet," he said, as he slid out of me.

I was floating on the swaying ocean as his warm lips covered my clit. He licked and sucked and hummed as the water carried me in its arms, rocking me back and forth, bringing me to the brink of bliss then he stopped.

"Come on," he said, as he led me out of the water.

His hand caressed my backside as he led me across the sand to an outdoor shower beneath the staircase. He turned on the shower and the warm water felt stingingly hot against my breasts. Within seconds, my body got used to the hot water as we rinsed the sand and saltwater off our bodies. His hands caressed my body, making certain there was no sand hiding in any crevices. He reached my slit and he stroked slowly as he looked me in the eye, watching my reaction.

My legs turned to jelly and he slid his arm around my waist to keep me from collapsing as he continued to gently rub my clit. I arched my back and he took my nipple into his mouth, sucking and nibbling, until I exploded with pleasure. He held onto me tightly until my body released a final shudder.

"Oh, my god," I said, as I tried to catch my breath.

He held tight to me, kissing and licking every inch of skin on my neck and shoulders until I regained my strength. His erection was stiff against my belly. I knelt before him and he plunged himself into my mouth. I held tightly to his ass as the tip of his cock hit the back of my throat. I pulled my head back and lightly kissed the tip, eliciting a pleasurable chuckle out of him.

"Oh, baby. Don't stop."

I took him fully into my mouth again as I slid my finger between his cheeks, caressing him. He groaned loudly and I took that as a sign to keep going. I bobbed my head faster as I slid my finger inside him.

CASSIA LEO

"Oh, fuck," he cried out, and his body shivered under my grasp.

I teased the tip of his cock again, licking and kissing the delicate ridge as I massaged the sensitive spot inside him. I took him into my mouth again, sucking and savoring every inch of him. He let out one more rapturous groan before he came. I swallowed his juices and licked my lips clean, relishing his delicious flavor, which I had grown to love.

"That was amazing," he said, as he pulled me up and buried his face in my neck. "I want to devour you. I want to feast on you every day for the rest of my life."

His hands roamed over my ass and I couldn't believe I still wanted more of him—and now.

"Let's take this upstairs," I said, as I grabbed his cock and he immediately became hard again. "Hubby."

He smiled as he placed his hand over mine. "As you wish, princess."

EPILOGUE

The mailman rang our doorbell at a few minutes past noon. I signed for the thick manila envelope and my heart jumped when I saw the return address.

"Chase! Honey! It's here!" I shouted from the bottom of the staircase.

No doubt he was upstairs in his office negotiating a large business deal, and I was most certainly interrupting him, but he told me that no matter what he was doing I was to notify him the moment this package arrived. Within seconds, Chase came tearing down the floating staircase, making it appear as if he were truly flying—my superhero. He tore the envelope from my grasp and savagely ripped it open. He opened the blue folder within and we skipped a bunch of unimportant stuff before we got to the most beautiful sentence I'd ever seen, and we both read it aloud.

"It is therefore ordered, adjudged, and decreed that the marriage relationship existing between Chase Allen Underwood and Katherine Ingrid Johnson should be and is hereby terminated and dissolved, both parties released therefrom."

We jumped up and down like massive dorks, unable to control our glee. "You know what this means, right?" I said, as he kissed the paper and tossed it to the floor so he could throw his arms around me.

"What does it mean?"

Chase knew I had been waiting for this day to come so I could finally start planning our *real* wedding, but things had changed since the day of our beach ceremony.

"It means that we can get married before the baby's born."

His eyes widened, but he remained silent. My heart sank deeper into uncertainty with every torturous moment I waited for his response.

"Chase? Say something?"

His posture relaxed as he took my face in his hands. "There's only one thing I want to say to you right now, and that's... thank you."

"Thank you for what? For being fertile?" I teased him.

"Well, besides that, thank you for giving me everything I ever wanted. Thank you for making this house feel like a home. Thank you for opening my eyes to what is truly important. And most of all...." He kissed my jaw and worked his way down my neck to my shoulder before he scooped me up into his arms. "Thank you for not wearing panties with that dress."

THE END

Continue onto the next page for a preview of Mirror (Luke #1) by Cassia Leo.

1

B e careful what you wish for, you just might get it… hard and fast. That was how my rise at NeoSys, Inc. happened. One day I was an intern for the Director of Marketing, the next I was the most trusted corporate spy working under the COO of the second biggest software company in America. Well, actually, we didn't call ourselves spies. My official title was Competitive Intelligence Officer.

I had worked for NeoSys for just over two years, since the last semester of my senior year at Cornell. NeoSys employed over 10,000 software engineers worldwide, creating everything from mobile phone software to virtual environments. We were second in the industry only to Maxwell Computers, and my job was to fix that.

I walked into the reception area at Maxwell Computers' corporate office in Seattle, trying to regulate my breathing as I anticipated my interview with Luke Maxwell: the hottest CEO in America, possibly the world. I swallowed my nerves as I passed a setup of sleek gray sofas on my way to the receptionist's desk. The glass ceiling in the lobby flooded the space with intense natural light and gave everything an unnatural glow, as if everything at Maxwell Computers shined with the light of God.

It seemed everything Luke Maxwell touched these days was blessed. Twenty-eight years old and he was the richest man in the country. People across the globe, from toddlers to seniors, were scrambling to get their hands on his latest products. All I wanted was to get my hands on the password for a software project he had dubbed "Blaze: The greatest innovation to hit the industry since the Internet."

The receptionist wore square glasses, which were half-covered by her long, black bangs. With her gray hoodie pulled over her head, she looked young enough to be in high school. She stared at me as I approached the desk as if she were trying to make me even more nervous.

"Hi, I'm Brina Kingston. I'm here for an interview with Mr. Maxwell."

She squinted at me for a moment before she answered. "You're Brina?"

"Uh, yes, I'm Brina. Is he expecting someone else?"

She looked me up and down a couple of times before she shook her head and touched her glossy white computer screen. The screen came alive and another woman's face flashed on; a woman I recognized. She was older, maybe late fifties, but she was impeccably made up with her hair in a neat twist and her makeup looking like it had been painted on by Hasbro. But she wore a plain black t-shirt, like the t-shirt the receptionist was wearing.

"Janice, the ten a m interview is here," the receptionist said and the fifty-some Barbie lit up with glee.

"Well, send her up. You know Mr. Maxwell hates it when we keep him waiting."

It seemed odd to me to hear an older woman calling twenty-eight-year-old Luke Maxwell "*Mr.* Maxwell."

The receptionist looked up then pointed at an elevator lobby to my right. "Twelfth floor."

"Thanks."

The two doors I passed on the way to the elevator were so glossy and white I could see my reflection. I reached the elevator and was not surprised to see myself again in the glass doors. I pressed the call button and resisted the urge to start adjusting my hair. The doors slid open and I stepped into the elevator. The walls and bottom of the elevator were also made of glass and I quickly grasped the handrail once I had pressed the number twelve button.

One look through the transparent floor at the cables beneath the elevator cabin and I closed my eyes. I hated elevators. I hated anything that forced me to climb higher than two feet off the ground. My brother's broken body flashed in my mind and I gritted my teeth against the image, but I could already feel the panic building as my heart raced and my mouth went dry.

A fucking glass elevator! Couldn't someone have told me this before I agreed to take this assignment? I bit my lip hard enough to draw blood as I tried to push out the thoughts of the day my brother chose a flying leap over one more tour of duty.

The elevator stopped and I kept my eyes level as I opened them so I wouldn't glimpse the hundreds of feet of empty space below me. The glass door slid open and I rushed out onto the polished concrete floor of level twelve. Barbie smiled at me from her pristine white desk a few yards away. Again, it looked odd to see this woman with her perfect hair and makeup wearing a t-shirt and jeans. I was beginning to feel out of place in my gray pencil skirt and silk oxford.

"Hi, I'm Brina Kingston," I said, being careful to keep my voice level and my shoulders back as I approached her, thoughts of my brother quickly evaporating into a cloud of anxiety over meeting Luke Maxwell.

"Hello, Brina. I'm Janice." We had to pretend we didn't know each other. "Mr. Maxwell is on a phone call," she continued. "He should be ready for you in just a few minutes. Please have a seat. Can I offer you something to drink? Water, coffee, diet soda?"

Diet soda? Was Janice implying I needed to go on a diet? I resisted the urge to inform her I had had multiple modeling job offers before I joined NeoSys two years ago at the age of twenty-one. One photographer called my breasts, "more luscious than a two scoops of vanilla ice cream." I wasn't a size zero, but no one had ever called me fat—except my brother when he really wanted to hurt me.

"No, thank you, Janice," I replied.

I had drunk half a gallon of water this morning in preparation of today's meeting. I didn't want my mouth to go all dry and crackly in the middle of the interview. I didn't expect to get the job on the first try—I already had my follow-up phone call scripted—but nothing could be left to chance today.

I took a seat in the cold, glossy white chair and set my purse on the chair next to me, fighting the urge to reach inside my purse and take out my Maxwell Flame phone. I told my boss at NeoSys that I had only bought the Flame for appearances, to nail the interview, but the truth was that it was far superior to the phones that used NeoSys software. If we didn't get our hands on Maxwell's newest software creation, we would lose all prospects at a half-billion-dollar deal with Imitex Robotics to develop the software for their new artificial intelligence line of products.

A soft pinging sound came from Janice's computer and she tapped the screen before she looked at me. "He's ready for you. You can go right in."

I grabbed my purse and headed for the glossy door behind her. I turned the lever on the door and the weight of the heavy door seemed to carry it open on its own. I stepped inside and panicked a bit when I didn't see Luke at his desk. I stepped farther inside and saw him standing at the far right end of the office near a wall of transparent floating shelves stocked with everything books to bottles of bourbon. He was pouring himself a glass when I caught his eye.

He seemed to be the only person in the office wearing business attire: a crisp shirt and slacks and a thin blue tie. He looked like he had stepped out of a Gucci ad. The morning sunlight poured in through the windows behind him and sparkled in his glass.

He placed the bottle of bourbon on a shelf and cocked his eyebrow; a simple gesture that made him appear even more gorgeous. "*You're* here for the interview?"

The inflection on *you're* confused me.

"I'm sorry, were you expecting someone else?"

He tilted his head at me as if he was the one who was confused. "Well, yes, I was expecting someone a bit... older."

My body tingled as he approached me with his glass of bourbon clinking in one hand, his other hand reaching into the pocket of his slacks. My gaze roamed over his perfect cheekbones and lips, mesmerized.

Come on, Brina. Say something.

"I... I can assure you I'm the most qualified candidate at the agency," I replied, with only a slight warble in my voice. "Joplin only farms out the best and brightest for their executive positions."

"Executive positions." He repeated this as if it meant something more and I suddenly had a weird image of Luke and I executing a few positions in my bed.

I tried not to blush at this thought, but I couldn't hold back my smile. "I *am* here to interview for the position of executive assistant, aren't I?"

He was just a couple of feet away from me now. With the glow of the sunlight behind him and the soft smile on his face he looked positively angelic. I wanted to reach out and stroke the light shadow of hair on his jaw.

He brought the glass to his lips and took a sip. "Have a seat."

Mental note: He drinks in the morning.

I exhaled slowly before I took a seat in front of his desk. He sat in the spinning silver chair on the other side and set his glass on the desktop. He spun around in his chair so he was facing the wall of windows.

"Why do you want to work here, Brina?"

I hadn't introduced myself yet, so that meant that Luke was good with names.

"At the risk of sounding like a groupie, I love Maxwell products and I really admire what you've done for the industry. I've wanted to work here since I was a freshman at Cornell."

It was all true. I had actually applied to Maxwell Computers before I applied to NeoSys, but NeoSys called me first and I was desperate to get my foot in the door. I never did hear back from Maxwell Computers on that internship and now I was glad for that. I probably never would have been promoted so quickly in a place like this.

"You don't sound like a groupie," he replied, though he was still staring out the window instead of looking at me. "You sound like me, only for me it was Microsoft. They rejected my application for an internship when I was seventeen, so I decided to build something of my own. Is that what you're trying to do here?"

"I'm not a software engineer."

"Are you trying to *build* something for yourself? Do you think you can get in good with me by coming in here looking like that?"

"What? I'm sorry, I'm not sure I'm following you."

He turned his head and glared at me from across the desk. I stared back at him, making sure to blink a few times so he didn't feel challenged. Finally, he smiled.

"You're hired."

My mouth fell open. "Just like that?"

"Come here. I want you to see something."

"Excuse me?"

"Come around the desk. I want to show you something."

I suddenly had a flashback of the time I caught a homeless man jerking off behind a Wal-Mart. I stood from the chair, leaving my purse behind, and circled the desk toward him. When I got behind his desk, I was pleased *and* disappointed to find him fully clothed. He pointed at the window and I followed the direction of his finger.

The view from his office was stunning. The city skyline rose up like monoliths against the serene blue of the Puget Sound.

"Do you see that boat out there?"

I squinted through the bright morning light and searching the ocean until I saw what looked like a modest sail boat floating on the water.

"The sailboat?"

"If you want this job you're going to have to promise me one thing."

Great. This was where the most private bachelor in America made me his next conquest. He gazed up at me from where he sat with one eyebrow cocked awaiting my response.

"What do I have to do?"

"You have to promise you won't get sick on my boat."

"I love boats."

The corners of his lips turned up in a cunning smile that made my breath stutter. "I hope you brought your sea legs because we're heading out to the marina now."

OTHER BOOKS BY CASSIA LEO

LUKE Series **(Erotic Romance)**
Relentless **(New Adult Romance)**
Shattered Hearts #1
Pieces of You **(New Adult Romance)**
Shattered Hearts #2
Bring Me Home **(New Adult Romance)**
Shattered Hearts #3

Coming Soon....

Abandon **(a spin-off of the Shattered Hearts Series)**
Black Box **(a stand alone new adult romance)**

ABOUT THE AUTHOR

New York Times and *USA Today* bestselling author Cassia Leo loves her coffee, chocolate, and margaritas with salt. When she's not writing, she spends way too much time watching old reruns of *Friends* and *Sex and the City*. When she's not watching reruns, she's usually enjoying the California sunshine or reading—sometimes both.

CPSIA information can be obtained at www.ICGtesting.com
Printed in the USA
LVOW07s1416190114

370046LV00003B/219/P